BOOK 2:
OUT OF THE
SHADOWS

BOOK 2:
OUT OF THE SHADOWS

tim
bowler

philomel books / an imprint of penguin group (usa) Inc.

First American Edition published 2010 by PHILOMEL BOOKS. A division of Penguin Young Readers Group. Published by The Penguin Group. Penguin Group (USA) Inc., 375 Hudson Street, New York, NY 10014, U.S.A. Penguin Group (Canada), 90 Eglinton Avenue East, Suite 700, Toronto, Ontario M4P 2Y3, Canada (a division of Pearson Penguin Canada Inc.). Penguin Books Ltd, 80 Strand, London WC2R 0RL, England. Penguin Ireland, 25 St. Stephen's Green, Dublin 2, Ireland (a division of Penguin Books Ltd). Penguin Group (Australia), 250 Camberwell Road, Camberwell, Victoria 3124, Australia (a division of Pearson Australia Group Pty Ltd). Penguin Books India Pvt Ltd, 11 Community Centre, Panchsheel Park, New Delhi—110 017, India. Penguin Group (NZ), 67 Apollo Drive, Rosedale, North Shore 0632, New Zealand (a division of Pearson New Zealand Ltd). Penguin Books (South Africa) (Pty) Ltd, 24 Sturdee Avenue, Rosebank, Johannesburg 2196, South Africa. Penguin Books Ltd, Registered Offices: 80 Strand, London WC2R 0RL, England.

Printed in the United States of America.
Design by Richard Amari.
Text set in Charlotte Book.

Library of Congress Cataloging-in-Publication Data
Bowler, Tim. Blade : out of the shadows / Tim Bowler.—1st American ed. p. cm. Summary: Badly injured, fourteen-year-old Blade must continue to use his exceptional "street smarts" and waning strength to outsmart dangerous thugs while he considers surrendering to the police to face the consequences of a past he has tried to forget. [1. Street children—Fiction. 2. Violence—Fiction. 3. Murder—Fiction. 4. Gangs—Fiction. 5. Homeless persons—Fiction. 6. England—Fiction.] I. Title. PZ7.B6786Bko 2010 [Fic]—dc22   2009003155

ISBN 978-0-399-25187-0
10 9 8 7 6 5 4 3 2 1

For Rachel
with my love

BOOK 2:

OUT OF THE
SHADOWS

1 EVER WONDERED WHERE YOU GO when you're dead? Then watch this space. Cos I've been there. And here's something to blitz your mind.

I'm still there.

And I might not be coming back.

It's out of my control now. I can't make anything happen in this place. It's just me and Death. And you don't mess with him. He's the gobbo in charge.

But what's it like? I'll tell you, Bigeyes.

First up, no lights or heavenly voices. None of that stuff. What you get is memories. It's just like they say. They come flashing past. They're like pictures.

They're doing it now. Pictures of people, places, stuff you've done. Your life like a movie spinning through you. And that's where it hurts.

Cos I don't want to see mine.

Or most of it. Maybe bits. The times with Becky.

Now don't get confused, cos there's two Beckys, right? Sweet and sour. There's the one who died. That's sweet Becky. And there's the one who should have died. The sour one— the troll, the dreg.

The one who zipped me over and told me little Jaz was her daughter when she wasn't. I got lots of names for that troll. But we'll call her Bex, all right? So you don't get stumped in the head. Cos you get stumped easy, don't you, Bigeyes?

Becky and Bex, sweet and sour. Got it?

I've been seeing pictures of sweet Becky. Her beautiful face, those eyes. Her hair used to shine. Did I ever tell you that? And it had this kind of smell. Sort of fragrant.

Even the day she died she smelled like a flower. And looked like one.

I miss her, Bigeyes. She's the only picture I want to see in all these memories. But I got no choice about that. I got to deal with the rest of 'em too. And they're coming thick as rain. Death's one busy gobbo.

And here's something else.

They don't all make sense. It's weird, Bigeyes. All this stuff, all these pictures—they're kind of cloudy. I thought everything would be clear in Death's little snug.

But it's not clear at all. I'm seeing things I remember and yet I don't remember. Does that make sense? Like they're memories but they're not. Things I've done only I've forgotten.

'Specially the early stuff.

That's the stuff that's really hard to see. I can see bits but lots of it's sort of shadowy, like it's almost a memory but not quite. Maybe that's a good thing. I've never liked remembering.

But at least it's not jumping about. It comes in the right order. Starts with Day One. And here's the first problem. Cos Day One's a shadow. Can't remember Day One, can't see it clear. But I can feel it. And that's the second problem.

Cos it was trouble. I'm telling you, it was trouble.

That's right, Bigeyes. The bad stuff started on Day One.

Don't ask me how I know.

And the pictures keep coming. Age one, age two, age three

and on they go. I don't like to watch 'em but they keep coming. They just won't stop. He's one mean gobbo, this Death.

Age seven.

I'm standing on the pedestrian crossing, stopping all the traffic, swearing at the drivers. Only now, when I see it flashing in front of me, it's not like I remember it. What's different is me.

I'm different.

Cos I'm not just a seven-year-old kid in this picture. I'm a kid who's lived for seven years. And that's not the same thing at all. Not when I've just watched those seven years again and seen what's in 'em, and who's in 'em, and what happened.

And there's shadows in there too, stuff I can't see, stuff I've blocked out and don't want to remember. Or maybe it's stuff that's blocked me out. Don't know. Doesn't make much difference.

It's bad anyway.

I'm seeing that kid on the pedestrian crossing like I'm watching someone I never knew before. Only there's no time to think about it. Cos there's more pictures coming.

Age eight, and then the change, the big change. If it was bad before, it's worse now. New places, new faces, new dangers. Big new dangers. Only I'm getting dangerous too. You better believe it. I'm getting dangerous too.

And I'm starting to like it.

Age nine, age ten. It changes again. I meet Becky, sweet Becky. Good pictures at last, only more dangers too, more faces. I can see most of 'em now. Not many shadows here. It's the stuff before seven that's cloudy. This later stuff's easy to see.

And I don't like it.

I almost prefer the shadows. They're bad news but at least I can't see what they are. These other pictures—I can't miss 'em. Each one's like the knife Trixi's brother stung in my head.

And they're coming too fast. I want to tell Death to slow down, only I don't dare. Like I say, you don't mess with this gobbo.

Age ten. Yeah, I'm still seeing age ten. It's taking time to run through. That's cos so much happened in it. Too much. I'm starting to hurt, starting to want out. I'm starting to lose it. Only good thing is Becky.

Then I lose her too.

Age eleven. When it came to a head, when it all got too much. And then I'm gone.

Only I'm not. I've run away, left the old place far behind. I've moved to the city and I'm playing dead. I thought it was a good idea. But I should have known better. It was a dimpy idea. It worked for three years.

But they were always going to find me.

You can't play dead with these gobbos. The only dead for them is real dead. And you don't play it. Cos dead's not a game. Not with them.

The pictures keep coming. Lots of 'em now. Like the closer I get to when the knife plugged me, the better I see stuff. Maybe it's just cos it's more recent. Don't think so though. Death's not fussy how he gives you stuff. He just blams it in your face. And right now he's spinning more than I can keep up with.

There's the places in the city, places where I slapped it,

living rough on the streets, before I found my snugs. Duffs I hung around with in alleys, doorways, hovels, ruins, finding out where they went.

Then finding my own way.

The houses and flats and other places I snugged out in. I got pictures of all of 'em rushing through my head. And all the nebs I saw. The slugs I kept away from in the city, the gangs who caught up with me.

Like Trixi's lot.

And then Mary. Old white-haired Mary with her crazy dog. And here's another thing about Death, Bigeyes. He's not fair. You'd think now that he's got me he'd tell me what happened in the bungalow that day.

Only no.

Like I say, he's one mean gobbo.

He shows me the house again, and the gobbos. I can see 'em forcing their way in. Paddy and his mate, and the fat man, the hairy grunt. I can see myself running away. I can hear the gunshots again.

Bang! Bang!

Two of 'em, loud in my brain. Only I still can't see what happened in the bungalow. Why won't Death show me that?

Cos he's too hot with buzzing the next picture at me. Trixi's body lying on the floor. Paddy leering in the doorway. Sour Bex smashing the window, and me and her running away.

And I still don't know what happened to Mary. Cos everything's moving again. It's me and Bex and now little Jaz. I don't know she's Trixi's daughter. Bex's told me the kid's her own. Only Bex was lying.

And the pictures keep coming. Bex disappears, Jaz disappears. I find 'em again, only I find the girl gang too. And Riff. And Dig, the big guy, Trixi's brother, the guy with the knife.

And the gobbos are still after me. Paddy's gone but there are still five left. And I'm wounded now. Dig's knife's ripped up my forehead and I'm blacking out. And here's where everything turns dark.

What do I remember at the end?

A knife moving, cool as a breeze. A hot pain singing in my head. The trolls in the girl gang screaming. Riff standing back, Dig grinning. The whole crowd bundling me onto the bank, leaving me by the river. The stumble to the warehouse, the gobbos closing in.

A thought fluttering in my head. I'm fourteen and I'm going to die.

Fourteen.

Darkness. Then gunshots.

Bang! Bang!

Two of 'em. Like the time at the bungalow. And then the voice.

It speaks my name. The name sweet Becky gave me long ago. Only the person speaking doesn't know that name. I know that cos I recognize the voice. It's the last thing I remember before this. And I'm freaking out, Bigeyes.

Cos the voice is speaking again now. I can hear it right this moment. Speaking my name like it did before.

"Blade," it says.

And I'm feeling this shiver.

Cos the person speaking my name is dead too.

2

"BLADE," SAYS THE VOICE.

It's Mary. Old white-haired Mary with the crazy dog. But Mary's dead.

"You're dead," I murmur.

"As dead as you are," comes the answer.

Silence, sort of. No more voices, just the buzz of my thoughts. Then another sound. Kind of a low rumble. Can't make it out.

"You're dead," I say again.

She doesn't answer this time. But there's still this rumble. It's not loud, just a weird blur of a sound. Something's moving too. Maybe it's me.

It's not me. It's something else.

Only I'm moving with it.

The pictures have stopped. Just darkness now, and I'm starting to wonder about death. More darkness, more rumbling. Is this it? Am I going to lose it now? Maybe that wasn't death before. Maybe it was just the way in. And now the door's closed behind me, and there's no light inside.

Or maybe . . .

Another voice, some gobbo. He's murmuring something. No, he's not. He's shouting. Just sounds like he's murmuring cos he's a long way away. He's shouting something but I can't hear the words.

Or is it me that's far away? Cos I don't know where I am,

Bigeyes. I'm blown away somewhere and I'm scared. It's like I'm in a million pieces. They're all so tiny I can't see 'em. Or maybe there's no pieces at all. Maybe I'm nothing. Maybe I don't exist.

Then it happens. The jolt, the pain, the explosion. The blinding light in my head, the picture flooding my eyes. The inside of an ambulance, two medics leaning over me, black gobbos.

Mary.

Then darkness again and a rush of thoughts. And pain everywhere, digging into me.

"Ah!"

Someone's screaming.

"It's all right," says a voice.

Another scream. Shit, it's me.

"It's all right," says the voice again. "We'll get you there."

One of the gobbos talking. But now I can hear Mary again.

"Blade." She's speaking soft, right in my ear. "You're going to be okay."

I got questions banging my head now, pricking my brain worse than the wound itself. She's used that name again. And I never told her it. What's going on?

I'm thinking back to when the knife got me. I can see the old hulk by the river. I can see Bex tied up. I can see the girl gang. I can see Tammy and Sash, and Xen and Kat. I can see dead Trixi's brother, the big guy, Dig. And Riff, his slimy mate.

But I'm moving on already. I can see little Jaz in the cabin, screaming cos she's terrified of me. And then the knife, splitting the air, splitting my head. Blood filling my eyes. Like it's doing now.

"Blood! Blood!"

"Easy, boy."

The man's voice again. Calm-sounding gobbo. Only what can he do? I thought I was dead. I almost was. I almost am. They won't get me out of this. I'm drifting off. They won't get me back. No way.

Another jolt, another explosion, another blinding pain.

Tight round my chest. I'm screaming, sitting up, eyes open. I'm peering at faces and they're peering back. I can see the front of the ambulance, the gobbo driving, some woman next to him, turning round. I can see the medics close, edging me back down.

And Mary.

And now more faces. Only they're not here in the ambulance. I know it. They're not real. I'm seeing Becky from the past, beautiful sweet Becky. And little Jaz. And then Bex.

"Not you, troll!" I scream.

"I'm here," she answers.

"Not you!"

"Blade—"

It's not Bex talking. It's Mary.

And I'm slumped back again, pain still pounding. It's getting worse. I'm moaning now. Can't drift off and I want to. I want to blast out somewhere else. Don't care where. Long as it's somewhere well dead.

I can feel hands touching me. Hate that, hate hands. And they're bringing the pictures back.

"Ah!"

"We're losing him." One of the gobbos, talking fast. "Quick!"

More hands. Something clammed over my mouth. It's going dark again. Sound of a siren growing loud.

Growing soft.

More darkness. Voices talking all at once, but they're low now. Can't even make out the words. Just know they're talking about me. Why's the pain still there if I'm drifting off?

Cos I am drifting off.

And it's good. It's a stinger. Like when I fold up in a blanket in some snug, and I know the owners aren't coming back, and it's my house, my little place, for another few hours, and I can rest, and forget, and not be me.

Not be Blade.

So why's the pain still there? It's meant to go when you die. You lose your body, you lose your pain. But I've lost my body and I still got the pain. And it's getting worse.

Now the noises are coming back. The voices, and they're not talking low. They're yelling. And the siren. That's yelling too. Everything's yelling. Even I'm yelling. That's right. I'm yelling and yelling and yelling. Cos suddenly I know what I really want.

I want life, Bigeyes. I want it back.

And I want it now.

3 BLACK SILENCE. THAT'S RIGHT. Black. It's got a color.

And everything's changed again. I'm somewhere else. Only I don't know where. All I know is it's black. And it's quiet. And I'm awake in my head. You better believe it. I'm wide-awake.

I'm watching cute, listening cute.

The black silence goes on falling. No voices, no sirens, no engines. No breathing even. I listen for my own. Can't hear it. But I can feel my chest moving. And the flicker of my eyes as they search the darkness.

Nothing.

Just black silence.

And me, thinking.

I'm lying down somewhere. I've worked that out. Don't know where. In a hospital maybe. They must have been taking me somewhere in that ambulance. Got to be a hospital. Only it doesn't feel like one.

The memories have come back again. Only they're different now. Or they look different. They were rushing past me before. But maybe that's cos I was dying. Now they're just floating in my head. I can't even see 'em really. There's too much darkness. I can just feel 'em moving like clouds.

And I'm starting to wonder again if I'm dead after all.

"Blade," says a voice.

I tense up. It's Mary speaking. And she's close.

I feel something, a hand. It's touching my arm. Don't like it. Try to move my arm, flick the thing off. It's no good. Can't shift a muscle. But the hand goes away.

And the voice comes back.

"You've been badly hurt," she says. "A knife slash across your forehead and very deep. The doctor says it cut your temporal artery. They've fixed that but you lost a lot of blood. Your clothes were so drenched they've had to destroy them. But at least you're alive."

"Where am I?"

"In a hospital."

"Who else is in the ward?"

"Just you and me."

"No other patients?"

"No, you've got it all to yourself."

"It's dark."

"You've got a bandage over your eyes."

More silence. I'm glad of that cos my brain's working again. Not fast, not yet. But it's working. And I know it's bad. I'm alive, okay. I'm in a hospital. But I can't move. So I'm still dead dung.

There's too many nebs want me grilled, Bigeyes. And don't tell me Mary's the only one who knows I'm here. What about Lenny and the grunt and the others? They got to be somewhere close.

I got to find out what happened. And I got to do it quick before I get rubbed out.

"You called me Blade," I say.

My voice sounds like someone else's.

No answer. But I know Mary's still there. I can feel her close by. So why's she not answering? I hear a movement.

Someone's joined her. I don't like this. Reach up, try and get rid of the bandage.

"Stop that." Another voice, a woman, brisk, cheery. Got to be a nurse. "I'll take off the bandage if you want me to. Just don't pick at it. And you're not to move your other arm at all. There's a needle in it with the drip attached."

I don't answer. I'm just glad my arm's moving again. I thought for a moment I couldn't shift it.

"Now then," says the woman.

Another touch on my arm, firmer than Mary. I feel my hand placed on the bed. Then a faint light round my eyes. But not much. Even with the bandage off, it feels dark.

"Can you see us?" says Mary.

Just about. Nurse leaning over me, Mary sitting by the bed. They look like ghosts. Maybe I do too.

"Can you take off the drip?" I murmur.

Nurse shakes her head.

"We'll keep it there a bit longer. It's not essential now that you're out of the high-risk zone, but we'll leave it in for the moment just to be on the safe side. So don't fiddle with it, okay?"

"How long have I been here?"

They look at each other, like they don't know which one's meant to answer. Nurse draws up a chair next to Mary. I don't want this. I want Mary on her own. I got to know what happened. And how much time I got before they come for me.

Mary answers.

"They rushed you in yesterday. Operated on you straight-away and gave you a blood transfusion. You've been uncon-scious most of the time since."

It's hard keeping my eyes on 'em. The lids keep falling

down. I'm aching all over now, 'specially my forehead. I almost want the nurse to put the bandage back. But I can't let her. There's too much to do.

I got to think.

Yesterday, Bigeyes. I've been here since yesterday. I remember the ambulance, sort of, but not the operation. Or anything since. That's bad, I'm telling you. What's been going on while I've been lying here blacko? Who else has looked in on me apart from Mary?

And who's waiting outside for me when I come out?

I got to get out of here. And I can't just blast out. First, I'm not strong. Second, I got to play stealth anyway. Got to sneak out. Trouble is, how weak's my body? I can move my arms and head. But what about the rest of me?

I haven't even tried standing up.

"You need to rest," says the nurse.

"I want to talk." I nod toward Mary. "To her."

"In the morning. When you've slept a bit more."

"I want to talk to her."

I feel my eyes close. I try to keep 'em open but it's no good. They close on their own. I hear my voice still speaking.

"I want to talk to her."

Then Mary's voice.

"I'll talk to him for a bit. Since he wants to. If that's okay."

"He's falling asleep," says the nurse.

"No, I'm not," I say.

"I'll stay with him anyway," says Mary. "If that's okay. Just for a few minutes."

Sound of a chair moving. I hope it's the nurse going, not Mary. I don't open my eyes. I just wait. Hand on my arm again. Feels like it did before. It's Mary's hand. I can tell. Still don't like it but I'm glad it's there. I'm glad she's there.

I keep my eyes closed.

"Mary?"

"Yes, sweetheart?"

"Is it nighttime?"

"Pretty much. Well, late evening anyway."

"Feels dark."

"It's certainly dark outside. Cold too, even for November."

The hand on my arm moves, strokes the skin. I give a flick and the hand goes away.

"You don't like being touched," she says.

I don't answer. Not sure it was a question anyway.

I'm thinking faster now. I'm tired all over but I'm not going to sleep, whatever the nurse thinks. I'm too scared for that. I got to know stuff. I got to find out what to do. And I got to find out soon or I'm cooked.

"What happened at the bungalow?" I say.

4

SHE TALKS QUIET but not just for me. She's got secrets of her own. I remember that from the bungalow. She was keeping lots back then. I like her voice, always did. Soft, Irish. Still don't trust it though. She called me sweetheart just now but she's also called me Blade. I keep my eyes closed and listen.

"They killed Buffy," she says. "Those men. She was barking at them and snarling and snapping her teeth. I tried to hold her back. I knew they'd kill her if she went for them."

"And she did."

"Yes. I couldn't stop her. She wasn't my dog, you know. She was a stray. I picked her up on the road a few days before I met you. Or maybe she picked me up. Not sure which. We just hit it off. Suited each other, I guess. I don't think she realized how grateful I was to have a rottweiler for a friend."

"Which one of 'em killed her?"

"The fat man."

That must have been the gunshots, Bigeyes.

"He just pulled out a knife," says Mary, "and let her jump onto it."

Shit, it wasn't the gunshots.

"I keep seeing that man's face," she says.

So do I, Bigeyes. I'm seeing it right now. I had that grunt in front of me when I was lying outside the warehouse. I could have pissed his life away. I had a knife, just like him, and he was square on, easy plug. Could have split him with one throw.

But he's still alive. And I'm stuck here.

And I still don't know about the gunshots.

Mary's talking again.

"That's what did it. Buffy getting killed."

She falls quiet for a moment, then goes on.

"So I pulled out my gun—"

"You what!"

"I pulled out my gun and fired it, twice. Once as they came forward, once as they ran away."

"Christ!"

"Keep your voice down." She lowers hers even further. "I'm not supposed to have a gun."

I keep my mouth shut, try to think. Don't know what to make of this woman. I knew she was zipping me over that time in the bungalow. Most of what she said was lies. But I didn't know she was dangerous.

I open my eyes again. Got to keep her in view. She's sitting close. Who the hell is she?

"Green eyes," I murmur.

"What's that?"

"You got green eyes."

"Can you see them in the darkness?"

"No."

But I remember 'em, Bigeyes. And how they watched me in the bungalow. Like they're doing now. Missing nothing. Figure appears in the doorway, that nurse checking. Mary sees me looking and turns her head.

"We're almost done," she calls out.

"Couple more minutes," says the nurse, and leaves.

Mary looks back.

"Where'd you get a gun?" I say.

"Doesn't matter." She pauses, like she's not sure if she wants to talk, then, "It's just for show, something I keep for protection. It's only got blanks in it. I wouldn't want to hurt anyone."

I would, Bigeyes. The grunt for starters. And his mates. And a good few other nebs.

"I'd never fired it before that time in the bungalow," she says. "But then I had to use it again—"

"Outside the warehouse."

"Yes."

It's falling into place, sort of. I remember the gunshots when I was lying on the ground with my head sprung. I thought I'd been shot. But I was out of my brain by then. Out of my body, out of everything.

But there's still questions.

How did she find me? How did she know my name? She's not one of the dregs out looking for me, or the mean-crack gobbos who sent 'em, or any of the other grudgy scumbos who want a piece of me. But she's no muffin either.

I got to be careful with this one.

She's talking again, still low but faster, like she knows the nurse is coming back any second. I'm glad. I want to hear.

"The men ran out of the bungalow. I don't know where they went. But I knew I had to get out quick. They could come back any moment. They wouldn't be scared of an old woman for long. They'd regroup and come back."

She's breathing fast now.

"I picked up Buffy and carried her out into the garden. There's a small tree at the bottom and some softer ground to the right of it. I dug a quick grave and put her in it, and covered it over. Then I got my things from the bungalow and hurried out."

"Where to?"

"Doesn't matter." Her voice sounds sharp for a moment. But it soon softens again. "You don't need to know where I went. I was a bit confused anyway, at first. A bit scared."

"But you phoned the police."

"Not straightaway."

She goes quiet again, in spite of the nurse coming back. I want her to spew some more. There's loads I got to know. She didn't phone the porkers. Why not?

I already know, Bigeyes.

"You're on the run," I say.

She doesn't answer.

"You are," I say.

"You don't know that. You don't know anything about me."

"I know that wasn't your bungalow."

She looks away. I feel slightly guilty. She's helped me—more than once. She's probably even saved my life. I shouldn't push her. She hasn't got to tell me stuff. I'm not going to tell her stuff.

"Thanks," I say.

She looks back at me. Her face is still dark but I can see the eyes moving. She doesn't believe me. Don't blame her. I wouldn't believe me if I was her.

"I mean it," I say.

She doesn't answer. Just goes on looking. I prompt her.

"Can you tell me some more?"

She glances over her shoulder.

"She's not there yet," I say.

I've been watching for the nurse too. Mary goes on checking, then turns back to me.

"I phoned the police," she says. "But I didn't do it that day. I was in too much of a state. I should have had the nerve. I might have saved that poor girl's life."

I don't answer. I just wait. I want her to finish. I want her to say everything.

"I rang the next day," she says. "I didn't give the police my name. I'm not telling you why. I just described the men. By that time the news had broken about that girl's murder in the bungalow. What was her name? Trixi Kenton. And your description was going round." She pauses. "I didn't say I'd seen you."

"Okay."

"Does that mean 'thank you'?"

I don't answer. She waits a moment longer, then goes on.

"But I met this girl."

It's got to be Bex.

"Down by the river," she says.

"What did you go down there for?"

"Never mind. I had my reasons." Mary pauses again. I catch a glint of green in her eyes. Then the darkness swallows it. "I was there anyway. And I saw you down the path. You were staggering across it onto the waste ground and you were streaming blood. Then you headed for the old warehouse."

I don't believe this, Bigeyes.

"And there were these men," she says. "I didn't know most of them, but I recognized the fat man and one of the others. They were following you toward the warehouse."

I still don't believe this. There's no way an old woman would follow those gobbos. Not to try and rescue me.

"I was going to turn and find a policeman," she goes on. "I'd seen a couple farther down the quay. But then this girl—"

"Bex."

"She didn't give her name. She just climbed out of one of the old hulks by the riverside and came racing up to me. She was in a terrible state. Said we had to do something or those men would kill you. And she told me your name. She said you were called Blade."

I close my eyes and listen on. And now I'm stinging inside. Cos you know what, Bigeyes? I owe this old girl big-time.

Again.

Cos she came on after me all by herself. Bex ran off, like she would, but the old girl came on, and found me with the gobbos, and pulled out that crazy gun again, and fired it.

Two gunshots.

One for each time she's saved my life.

5

THE NURSE IS TALKING.

"Lily, that's enough. Let him rest now."

Lily? Did you hear that, Bigeyes? The old girl's calling herself Lily. I don't believe it. And the nurse's drinking it up. She's something else, that Mary. Or whatever her name is.

I'm calling her Mary anyway. I told you once before—I don't give two bells about names. Mary speaks again, a whisper, dead close.

"Listen." She's talking fast, confidential, so the nurse can't hear. "I don't know why I'm saying this but . . . well, I'll say it anyway. I don't know who you are or what you've done. And I'm not asking. But I know you're in a heap of trouble."

She hesitates, then hurries on.

"If you ever need to find me, ask for Jacob at The Crown on South Street. I can't promise to help you. But I can promise to listen. And you keep what I've just said to yourself, okay?"

"Lily." The nurse again, all bossy. "That's enough now."

There's a silence. I wait for a bit, peek out the corner of an eye. Mary's gone but the nurse is still there. Sees me watching.

"You need to sleep," she says. "We can talk again when you've had some more rest." A pause, then, "But can you just tell me what your name is?"

I close the eye, act dozy. Nurse goes on.

"Lily didn't know and no one else does either."

I don't answer.

"Is it Slicky?" she says. "I mean, is that your nickname?"

Slicky. What Trixi and her crew called me.

I go on acting sleepy. Nurse doesn't speak again. I feel her tuck the sheets, linger for a bit, slip out. I keep my eyes closed, peer up at the lids. They feel heavy, like my thoughts.

I'm struggling, Bigeyes, struggling to think. But I got to. And I got to act. I just wish Mary had had longer. There's more I need to know. Though I can guess most of what happened outside the warehouse.

Mary fires the gun and clears out the gobbos. They wig it out of sight. Sound of the shots attracts the police. Mary puts the gun away before they turn up, says she didn't see anything, just heard the shots and found this boy lying wounded. Porkers call the ambulance and here I am. Mary comes with 'em.

No one's linked her and me. She's just some old bird who was on the spot at the time. That's why she's been allowed in to see me. Bex blasted off somewhere else. Like she would.

Who knows?

Whatever story Mary's told, they've bought it. Only now they're guessing I'm the boy called Slicky who's been on the news. So there'll be porkers in the hospital corridor waiting for me to come round.

And they're the nicest of the nebs I got to lose. I don't even want to think about the grinks waiting. They'll all know where I am now. How many of 'em are outside? And how many have slimed in?

I got to get out of here.

Wait a bit, listen cute, open my eyes, check round. Empty ward, lights off, except down the corridor. Sit up, check round again. Brain's swimming. I feel weak, dizzy, choked up. Head's pounding where Dig's knife fizzed me.

But I can think. I can feel. And what I feel is fear.

They're close, Bigeyes. They're all around us.

I got to do this, no matter what state I'm in. Pull back the sheet, edge my feet onto the floor, test my weight. Shit, I'm swaying. I'm standing but I got no balance. And I still got this effing drip in my arm.

Back on the bed, breathing hard, half sitting, half lying. I'm shaking like a dungpot. Got to get a grip. Got to think what to do. If I can't move, I'm drummed.

Footsteps.

Down the corridor.

Glance toward the door. No one there but someone's close. It's not the nurse. I can tell. Check round the room. There's got to be something I can use as a weapon if I need one. Cos I'm telling you, Bigeyes, the nebs who want me won't fuss over a hospital. They want me too bad for that.

Footsteps getting louder. There's more than one person.

Two, maybe three.

No weapon, nothing I can use. Got to hope it's just staff. No other choice. Back into bed, pull the sheets over, close my eyes again, almost. Peep out. Watch the door.

Three gobbos looking in. They're not staff. I'm watching cute. Don't know if they've worked out I'm awake. But they're watching. They're standing there, looking in.

I don't know these guys. Don't think so anyway. Can't see 'em clear with the lights off. Could be okay. But I don't think so. They don't smell like muffins. They're not porkers either. I always know porkers.

Nurse's voice down the corridor.

"Can I help you?"

Gobbos turn round. Nurse speaks again.

"Can I help you?"

"We're looking for a friend," says one.

Cool voice, cultured. This guy's slick.

"A patient?" says the nurse.

"Yes. Is this the Neurology Department?"

"You've gone past it. Back down the corridor, turn right at the end and keep going."

"Thanks."

Sound of footsteps tramping away. Then more, heading in my direction. Nurse's face appears in the doorway. I close my eyes right up, breathe slow. Footsteps up to the bed. Feel her check me over, fiddle with the sheets. Voice in the doorway, a gobbo.

"Jenny? Do you know who those men were?"

"No, Doctor." Nurse goes on tucking in the sheets. "They said they were looking for a patient in the Neurology Department."

"Did you believe them?"

"No."

Neither did I, Bigeyes. They're grinks. And they'll be back.

Silence. I keep my eyes closed, listen, think. I can sense the doctor's still in the doorway. Nurse stops fiddling. But they're watching me dead cute, both of 'em. I can feel it. Keep my breathing steady. Got to sound asleep.

Then wig it out of here soon as they're gone.

Doctor speaks again.

"I'll ask staff to keep their eyes open. We can't have unauthorized people wandering about. How is he?"

"Not sure. I think he might have tried to get out of bed. The sheets were a bit of a mess when I came in just now. But maybe he just twisted in his sleep."

More footsteps drawing close. Got to be the doc. I can feel 'em still watching me. Doc speaks.

"Well, he won't get very far if he does try to get out of bed. Not with an injury like that and the amount of blood he's lost. He'll do himself serious harm if he tries to move. Let's hope he's sensible and doesn't do anything stupid."

Yeah, right, Doc. You've worked out I'm maybe not sleeping. Got your message. But it makes no difference. When you and Nursey are gone, I'm gone too.

Sound of footsteps, his and hers, back to the door, then they stop. No more sounds. Keep my eyes well closed. They're still there by the door, watching. Doc's no fleabrain. I can tell. And Nursey's nobody's dimp.

Trouble is, I got to be even more careful now. The porkers will already have told the staff to keep an eye on me. And now these two have worked out I tried to get out of bed. They'll be watching more cute than ever.

That's going to make it harder for me to get out. And it won't be enough to stop the grinks. Those three gobbos might not come back. But somebody else will. I got to wig it out of here—somehow.

Only I can't yet. I got to play stealth first. Got to wait a bit. Still no sound of footsteps from the door. Doc and Nursey are still watching. Keep my breathing steady, my eyes closed.

I can see Mary's face inside the lids. And Buffy's too. I'm sorry she got killed. She was one crazy dog, but I liked her.

And I've got that grunt on my list.

Footsteps at last. They're moving off down the corridor. It's a good sound. But I'm keeping my eyes closed a bit longer to be safe. Got to make sure they've really gone. Couple of minutes. Couple more. Should be okay now.

Ease up the lids.

"So you're awake," says a voice.

6

A HAND SPLATS over my mouth, a knife pricks at my throat. It's one of those gobbos, the one who spoke to the nurse.

Keep still. Nothing I can do. He's too strong and I'm too weak. He's going to rub me out or he's going to take me. One or the other. Can't stop either right now. So keep still.

Got to act like I'm blown out, like I'm no trouble. He might just hesitate and give me a slot. Keep my lids low, peer up. I can see the shape of him, just. No sign of the other two.

He leans down. He's wearing a doc's coat. Keep my eyes glazed. Make like I'm drugged, like I'm stumpy in the head. I might just get a chance to do something.

But there'll only be one slam.

Got to act like I got nothing in me. Then hit when I can.

His eyes are close to mine. He's drilling me, peering in. Roll my eyes, let 'em mist up. But I got a good shot of him now. Tall gobbo, thirty-odd, ice cold. Never seen him before today.

The knife's moving, stroking my throat.

He likes this. He's having fun. I stay glazed, go on acting limp. He keeps his other hand tight over my mouth, leans closer, whispers.

"Time to get you out of here."

And then he moves, fast. Hands flip back but before I can make a sound, he's got tape squeaked over my lips and round my cheeks. Next moment he's ripped the needle and drip out of my arm, and the knife's back over my throat.

He's chill, this gobbo. And he's a pro.

He checks the doorway. Nobody there, no sounds in the corridor. He looks back, gives a little grin. Strokes the blade over my skin, grabs me by the hair, eases my head up from the bed.

"No point acting," he murmurs. "You're wide-awake."

I keep my eyes glazed. Got to keep doing it, whatever he says. Got to make like I'm spaced. Got to bide my time, keep my strength, wait for the moment, take him by surprise. And it won't be easy. He's no dumflush dreg like Paddy's gobbos.

He sits me up, his eyes close to mine again. I can feel him peering hard. He's searching inside my head, trying to click onto me. I stay glazed, limp.

Feel a sudden shock.

My body jerks forward. Can't help it. I know what he's done. He's dinked me with the knife. Just a little one at the base of the spine to shake me up. And now he's peering inside my head again. Keep glazed, keep limp. Hang down in his arms.

He's not bluffed. He knows I'm playing dog-eye with him.

"Won't work," he whispers.

Another dink of the knife. I jerk forward again, into his arms. He pulls my head in close to his, and there's his eyes searching my skull again. Somehow I keep glazing back. He's getting impatient now. Or maybe he's starting to wonder a bit. Got to hope he is. Got to make him feel I'm no sweat. Got to squeeze a lapse out of him.

He straightens up suddenly, pulls me by the hair toward the edge of the bed, gets his arms round my legs and twists them so I'm sitting there, slopped over.

"Put these on," he mutters.

He's found some clothes. Or brought 'em.

"They should fit you," he says.

I slump back on the bed.

"Sit up." He's getting angry now. "Or I'll make you."

I don't move.

He yanks me upright again, his eyes dark. Whips the knife in front of my face, flints it from side to side, trying to make my eyes follow. Blade glints but I keep glazed.

Suddenly he flings me back on the bed. He's crouched over me, dead close, too close. I try to open my mouth. It's no good. Tape's on too tight. And now he's pulling off my hospital gown.

I hate this. I got pictures from the past flashing by. I want to squirm, fight back. But I got to go on playing dog-eye. Got to stay limp, stay like I don't know what's going on.

He's got the gown off me now. I'm naked on the bed, gobbo bent over me, knees either side of my body. And he's touching me again. Only thank Christ, not that other way.

But it's still bad.

He's pulling the shirt on me, and then the sweater, and the underpants and trousers, and socks and shoes. He's quick and clever, and suddenly I'm dressed and he's looking round at the door.

Still nobody there.

He's off the bed now, picking me up.

"Time to go," he mouths.

And he's carrying me toward the door.

I stay limp, let my arms hang loose. He doesn't bother about them. Feels confident he can handle me. And he can right now. I feel like I got no strength at all. I'm just hoping I can find enough to do the business if I get a chance.

And I got to make a chance.

Cos once he's got me outside the hospital, it's over.

He won't be working alone. I told you. There's lots of grinks after me. There's the ones who want to rub me out for what I did. The enemies of my enemies. And there's the ones who want me alive. But that's only so they can torture me for what they want to know. And when they got that, they'll rub me out too.

So either way, it's bad.

I got to do something, got to make a chance, got to find something in me to nail this guy. He's stopped at the door, checking round. Nobody in the corridor. He sets off down it, carrying me easy. I'm lolling in his arms now. But I'm thinking quick.

He can't take me out the main entrance. He's got to find a side way out. Maybe the way he trigged in. Question is: which way's he going? I never been inside this hospital till now. But I know the streets round it.

I know 'em good, Bigeyes. Like I know all the city.

I'm trying to think. Which way would I go if I had to sneak out of here? I already know the answer. But he's got a different agenda. He's going to meet his mates. He stops near the end of the corridor.

Voices farther down, round the corner. Move my hand a little, loose and swingy. Want to see if I can work it closer to his knife. He's still got it in his hand. I can feel the flat of the blade against my body as he keeps me close.

He senses the movement and I let my arm flop again. He

looks round at me, gives a little knowing smile, turns back toward the sound of the voices, then opens a door to the left.

Don't remember seeing this, but it's no surprise. I was blacko when I came in here. He carries me through the door, shuts it behind us, dead quiet. We're in another corridor. Moves down it to the end, turns right. Halfway down, another door.

He pulls out a key, slots it in, opens the door. Little storeroom with mops, pails, cleaning stuff. Bottles of this and that. White coats hanging on hooks.

And a dead body lying on the floor.

7

MIDDLE-AGED GOBBO, one of the cleaners maybe. Scumbo probably just wanted one of the white coats. Saw the gobbo inside the room, strangled him, changed coats, nicked the key. And now he wants to slip back into his old coat and stroll out of here like nothing's happened.

There you go—his own coat at the back. He's shoved one of those giant garbage bags on top. And I know why. He's going to stuff me inside it, so he doesn't look like he's carrying some kid. I'm thinking fast. It's got to be now. I got to wipe this guy in here.

Yeah, Bigeyes, I got to kill him. No other way. It's him or me. And I can't screw up like I did with Paddy. I got to do the business, just like I used to. Got to find what I once had and settle this thing. Or we're done.

We're done.

Good news is he's got to put me down to change his coat. Bad news is I hardly got any strength. It's like I said, Bigeyes— one slam. That's all I'm going to get.

If that.

He closes the door behind us, slips the key in the lock, turns it. He's holding me close again, peering into my eyes like before. He's trying one last time to fix me. But he can't get inside my head. I'm still playing dog-eye.

He's even more dangerous like this. Part of him's decided I'm too weak to hurt him. But part of him's wary. Which part's

33

stronger? That's the crack of it. If it's the first, I still got a chance.

If it's the other, he'll glue his eyes on me too tight.

He stiffens. He's made up his mind.

Stay limp, stay focused, stay ready. He's moving, slow, his left arm under my legs, the other clammed round my body. Knife's in his right hand, brushing my arm.

Stay still. Wait.

He bends down, slow, slow. He's watching me cute. I can feel his eyes burning me, even with mine half-closed. Floor's coming closer. It's touching my feet, legs, bum, back, head.

He lets go. I flop back, roll my arms to the side, loll my head. He stands over me like a shadow. He's looking down. I can feel it. He wants to kill me so much. I can feel that too. He doesn't want to keep me alive, take me back. He likes killing. I can smell it.

He's found me, he's got me. That's trophy number one. Trophy number two will be bringing me in. But he doesn't want that. Too much trouble. And not enough fun. He wants trophy number three.

Taking me out.

But he's not allowed. He's been told he's got to bring me in. So he's looking down right now, and he's hating me for that. For all his cool, he's boiling inside. He moves, just a little, his right leg lifting over me. He's stepping off, reaching for the shelf.

Rustle of coats changing. The crackle of the garbage bag. The right leg moving back where it was. He's standing over me again, looking down. I don't need to see him to know that. I can feel everything I need to feel right here, on the floor, eyes closed.

I can feel him watching, shifting his weight from foot to foot, checking me over, checking I'm safe. Another rustle of the bag. He's bending down. He's drawing close. He stops. He's thinking how to do this. Pick the kid up and drop him in the bag or bend down farther and roll him into it?

Wait. Listen. Get ready.

He's moving again, bending close. He's going to pick me up first. Another rustle as he lets go the bag. Left hand slips under my legs again. Right's still got the knife. I can feel the blade as he slides his hand over my arm.

I'm moving up again, closer, closer, closer to his head.

And then I turn.

Sharp.

My right hand thrusting for his face.

He's not ready. He doesn't catch my arm. I'm through his guard and his eyes have pricked wide. And that's good. They're my target.

I stab 'em with the only blades I got.

My fingers.

One in each eye.

Hard.

He gives a yell, flicks his head back, slaps his left hand over his face. But I'm on his right wrist now. I've got his little finger in one hand, thumb in the other. I jerk both ways.

Snap!

Snap!

He roars and lunges, but I'm too good at this. I got the knife, I'm on his back and the blade's moving over his throat.

But then it stops.

I've frozen—again. I'm clinging to him, his hair tight in

the squeeze of my hand, the knife in my other hard against his throat. A red drip's trickling down his neck.

It should be a river by now.

He should be on the floor, his eyes dimming up, his sick life pumping over his chest. But he's still standing. He's moaning from his broken finger and thumb, and he's trembling, sweating, waiting for the moment. He thinks I'm taking my time, making him squirm before I wipe him out.

He knows what I can do. He doesn't know I've lost it.

Not yet.

When he works that out, I'm dead.

He's still waiting. But he's picked something up. I can sense it. I can feel his mind starting to move, starting to hope. I got to snuff that out. Got to bluff things, play strong. Even if I can't kill him, I got to make out I can.

And find some other way out of this.

He speaks.

"Thought I'd be dead by now."

Low voice, checking me out. I stroke the blade over his throat. He stiffens, but not enough. He's not as scared as he was.

"Don't tell me you're losing it, boy."

Defiance in his voice now. I lock my legs round him, let go of his hair, rip the tape off my mouth, grab his hair again, jerk his head back.

"Ah!" he goes.

I push the blade hard against his throat. Another red drip trickles down his neck. I wait till he feels it, lean close to his ear.

"What's my name, Scumbo?"

He doesn't answer. He's panting, his eyes flicking at me.

"I said what's my name?"

"Blade," he breathes.

"Say it again."

"Blade."

"Louder."

"Blade, Blade, Blade."

"Carry me to the door."

He steps past the other guy's body, stops at the door.

"Turn round."

He turns, facing back into the room. I keep the knife hard against his throat. He's still not scared enough. I can feel him starting to crack me. He's working out why he's not dead. I got to move quick before he tries something.

"Down on your knees."

He doesn't move. He's testing me again. Got to act now or he'll have me.

Rasp the knife over his throat, scrape some of the blood onto the blade, hold it in front of his eyes so he can see it. He stiffens again, his eyes fixed on the knife. Whip it back to his throat.

"Down on your knees."

He drops to his knees, my legs still straddling him, the knife against his throat. I let go of his hair, reach back with my free hand, unlock the door, pull out the key.

"Lost the bottle, have you?" he says suddenly. "To kill me?"

There's mockery in his voice now. I lean close again.

"Kill you?" I run the blade up and down his neck. "Is that what you want, big man?"

He doesn't answer. I whisper into his ear.

"Put your hands behind your back."

He doesn't move. He's stiffened again, sweat pouring like before.

"You might regret that last remark, Scummy."

"Listen—"

"Put your hands behind your back."

He moves his hands slowly behind him. He's trembling again, but so am I now. I got to do this real quick. I jump off and kick him hard in the back. He falls forward and his face thuds against the floor. I slip out of the room, slam the door after me and lock it. From inside comes Scumbo's voice.

Hard, dangerous.

"You're dead, kid. You know that? Cos you've lost it. You couldn't kill Paddy. You couldn't kill me. You're finished. And you know it."

The door starts pounding and a crack appears round the lock.

8

DOWN THE CORRIDOR, quick as I can. Got to get out of here somehow. Problem is, all the strength I had went into nailing that gobbo. Don't know what I got left except fear. But maybe that's enough to shift me.

Least there's nobody here and no sound of voices or footsteps, just the pounding of the door behind him. He'll be out of there any second.

End of the corridor, through the exit.

Two more corridors, right and left. Three nurses halfway down one of 'em. Haven't seen me yet. Nobody in the other. Slip down that, stop at the door, check through the glass panel.

Another corridor, also empty.

Hope it stays like this. Cos you know what, Bigeyes? I'm starting to think of a way out of here. If I can just stay lucky and find the grit. I know what's waiting for me outside. Not just those two gobbos I saw with Scumbo.

There's all the others.

I'll never make it out any of the normal exits. Not in this state. Not even if I was crack-hot. All the exits'll be watched. But there's another way out if I can just get there. And if I can find my way back into the city, she'll take care of me. I got a snug not far away. Not one of the best but it'll do. If I can just get there, I can rest. And think.

But first we got to get out of the hospital.

Into the next corridor. I'm moving slow now. Every step feels tough and my head wound's hurting. Got to keep going. Still nobody here but I'm listening hard, watching cute. Drone of cars outside the hospital. Window ahead.

Slow down, ease close. Don't want anyone to see me from outside. Stop, peep through. Parking lot below. Dark, very dark. That's good and bad. Good cos they can't see me so easy. Bad cos I can't see them either.

Well, I can a bit. Enough lights to spot some of the nebs. Most of 'em are muffins. I can tell. Just people coming and going. I'm looking for the grinks. The ones not moving. They'll be out there. They'll be trying to look like muffins. But I'll know 'em.

There's one.

Over by the far end of the parking lot. Check him out, Big-eyes. See the ticket machine? Left of that. Got him? Gobbo in a long coat, lighting a cig. Standing by the Citroen. Looks like he's waiting for a friend. Only he's not.

He's waiting for me.

Another one farther to the right. Close to the ambulance bay. Tall gobbo, shiny forehead. Kind of guy who looks like he'd help anyone. Well, he wouldn't help me.

Come on. We can't hang about here.

Back from the window, crouch, creep past, on down the corridor. End's getting closer. Got to watch it. No door this time, just another corridor cutting past. And Scumbo's mates could be waiting round the other side.

Draw close. No sound of anything round the corner of the wall. No feeling of anyone. I usually know. I don't need to hear. I can feel if someone's there. Only that's when I'm strung right. I'm lugged in the brain right now, not thinking good. That's when I make mistakes. I got to watch extra cute or I'll crash my gut.

Stop at the corner of the wall.

Listen again. Nothing. Wait, try to feel what's round there. Why can't I do it? I used to feel, used to know. But I'm hurt too bad. Body's messed up, head's messed up. I'm trembling again.

Stick my head round the corner.

It's a risk but I'm desperate. And I'm lucky again.

No one there. Just another empty corridor. Door at the end, elevator to the right, emergency exit to the left. That's probably the way Scumbo was going to take me. Out the emergency exit and into the parking lot.

His mates'll be close by, most likely just outside. I got to be careful now. If they see me, I'm done. Trouble is, to do what I want, I got to get down to the end of that corridor.

Move. Make yourself do it.

Down the corridor, slow. Ease myself close to the wall. Here's the emergency exit. Just praying nobody's on the other side. They can't get in that way. But I'm still in trouble if they spot me.

Only chance I got to wig it is if no one sees me.

And that's asking a lot.

Least the corridor's still quiet. Here's the exit. I'm still hidden from the outside. But not for much longer. Creep forward, inch at a time. Glass window's in view. I can see the darkness outside and one tiny corner of the parking lot beyond.

No sign of any figures from here.

But I'm not up to the window yet. I'm at an angle. I'm still trembling and the pain in my head's growing worse. Reach up, touch my brow. Feels sticky. It's bleeding. I can feel it. That didn't come from fighting Scumbo.

That's my wound loosening up.

Another step toward the window, another, peep round, holding my breath. No one there. No one close anyway. But I can see the two gobbos farther down. Got 'em? One behind the Renault, one over to the right, behind the van.

Looking this way.

Just hope they haven't seen me here. They haven't moved. I think they're too far back to see clear. And the corridor's a bit dark behind the glass. Even so, I got to be even more careful with the next bit. Look to the right.

You got it, Bigeyes. We're taking the elevator.

Crouch right down, cheek against the floor. And now crawl. Even this is risky. I'm still visible through the emergency exit. And it's not just Scumbo's two mates I'm worried about. It's all the other grinks out there.

But I got no choice.

I got to crawl and hope.

Reach up, press the button for the elevator. I'm praying there'll be no one in it. Whirring sound, chink of a bell, clunk of the doors opening. I'm still lying here, hoping.

It's empty. Roll into the elevator, crawl to the side, out of the sight line from the emergency exit. Stand up, swaying. Spot of blood nicks the floor. Check my pockets. No handkerchief. Reach up, press my sleeve against the wound, hold it there, take it away. Cuff's all red.

But I can't be doing with that now.

Reach out, press the button.

Top floor.

9

DOORS CLOSE. Judder of the elevator as it moves. We're going up. I'm tracking the floors. Third, fourth, fifth, sixth. Praying no one'll get on. Elevator stops.

Sixth floor.

Damn, still three more to go. Turn my back on the doors, kneel down like I'm doing my laces. Hear the doors open, woman's voice out in the corridor.

"Can you help me?"

I don't look round.

"I said can you help me?"

Bit of a stewpot. I don't want to look at her. Voice comes again, angry now.

"Are you deaf or something?"

Then a gobbo's voice.

"Mrs. Baker, you're not supposed to be out here on your own."

I hear the doors closing again. Glance round. Old woman in a wheelchair, glaring in at me. Male nurse fussing over her.

"Mrs. Baker—"

"I want to go in the elevator."

"Mrs.—"

But the doors have closed and we're moving on. Only down again. Christ, Bigeyes, this is sticking me in. It wouldn't be so bad if I was strong. But I feel so weak, so useless. It's not just my body. It's my mind. I feel split inside.

I want to scream so bad.

And now the elevator's taking me back down.

Stops again. Third floor. This time I don't kneel down. This time I got to do something else. Doors open. Ancient gobbo standing there on his own, waiting to get in. Only I'm blocking the way.

"All right, Grandpa?" I give him a manic grin. "Coming in to join me, are you?"

He stares. Not sure what to do.

"Take you up or take you down, Gramps?" I give him a wink. "Make it down, Claphead. That's where I'm going."

He takes a step back. I press the button.

"See you round, Gramps."

Doors close. And the elevator starts to climb again.

Yeah, I know. Risky. But what else can I do? Can't hang around any longer. And I can't have anyone in the elevator. All I can do is hope the old boy'll keep quiet about it. And if he reports it, he might just say I was going down, not up.

They're going to see I'm gone anyway soon. They probably know already. There's no time to lose. Elevator's moving good. Keep going, keep going. Don't stop. It doesn't stop. It's moving, up, up, up. Three floors to go, two floors, one.

Ding!

Top floor. Doors open. Nobody out there, thank Christ. Hum of talk somewhere round to the left. Creep out. Doors close behind my back. Whirr of the elevator as it heads back down. Look right and left.

No wards up here, like I hoped. Never been here before. But I know what I want. It's not a choice I wanted to make, not being so weak. But it's the only one left. And if I'm going to die, I don't want it to be the grinks that get me, you know what I mean?

But I'm not dead yet, Bigeyes.

There's still a chance. If I can just find the strength.

Check round. Voices still coming from the left. Gobbos talking. No sign of anyone but a half-open door at the end of the corridor. That's fine, whoever you are, long as you stay in there. Creep round to the right. Narrow corridor, offices and stuff.

Where's the bit I want?

There.

Staff Only.

Door to the outside. Little twist of steps climbing up. Another emergency exit. Check round. Still no sign of anyone. That's one bit of good news. Thought I'd have to duck and slink. Over to the door, check round again.

Nobody.

Press the bar, open the door, close it behind me. Up on the roof. Wind blams me like a fist. Christ, Bigeyes, it's freezing up here. Head's swimming with pain now. I can't stay long up here. I got to move quick. There's nothing to be gained by hanging around.

Okay—two ways out. One bad, one worse.

But before we decide, we got to check things out. Now listen up, Bigeyes—I'm going to tell you something. That's right, another thing I haven't told you. Get over it. I said I've never been in the hospital before. That was true. But one thing I didn't tell you.

I've been on it.

That's right. I've been up here. Roof's a good place if it's warm and you got to keep out of sight. I used to come up here a lot when I first hit the city. Before I found my snugs.

Haven't come up for a good while. Haven't needed to. Got enough places to chill. But this was a good one in the beginning. And there's lots of other roofs to use. It's like a city of its own up here. And it's safer than down on the streets.

Once you know it, you can move easy. Cos I'll tell you something else—I can't run good, but I can climb. And I know how to get off this place. Two ways, like I said.

One would be a whack if I was well. But I'm not, so it's bad. More than bad—it's lethal. As for the other way, well, let's check it out. But I already know what I'm going to see.

Come on, Bigeyes. Let me show you how many friends I haven't got. Over to the edge, crouch down, crane over. Check it out. What do you see down there?

Nothing?

Look again. I know it's dark but look, keep looking. Go on—what do you see? Still nothing? You blind or something? There, far left. See the street running off the parking lot? That's Whiteacre Lane. How many figures do you see?

Christ, Bigeyes, you must be looking out your stump. Or maybe I'm just more used to this. I've been used to it all my life. Looking and finding. Knowing where the trash lives.

There, end of the street—one figure. Another one on Belton Avenue. Another one farther up. Another one round the corner of Nelson Drive. There'll be more in some of those cars.

Yeah, I know. You're thinking they're just figures, just nebs. Harmless little muffins living their muffiny lives. They're not, Bigeyes. They're grinks. I always know. And I haven't finished yet. Move on, round the side of the roof. Keep checking down.

See 'em?

More round this side of the building. Move on. More again. Count 'em. How many have you seen? I've seen twelve. And there'll be others. I'm guessing twenty-plus round the hospital. And there'll be more in the streets round about, case I get through the first crunch.

Don't shake your head.

They're grinks. They're from the past.

And they've come back.

That's why we can't use the exits. That's why we can't take the emergency steps down. So there's only one way left. As I expected.

Let's get it over with.

10

BACK END OF THE ROOF, away from the main entrance. Creep up to the edge. Check over. What do you see from this side?

Yeah, yeah, more buildings. That's just hospital stuff. What else? Playing fields beyond, okay. I'm not talking about them. Closer in. Check over the edge. Right over. Follow the wall down. What do you see?

More emergency steps.

That's how I used to get up here. Only we can't take 'em. Not all the way down. Too risky. There's grinks watching this part of the complex too. But we can take the steps a little way down. It might just be too high up for those dungpots on the ground to see us in the dark.

Got to try anyway.

Let's go.

Over the edge, foot on the step, another, then down. Wind's butting me bad now. I'm shivering, my head's still swimming and the pain's getting worse. My wound's shedding blood again. Can't stop to fiddle with it. Got to hold on, and this is the easy bit.

Twenty feet down, twenty-five, thirty.

Stop.

Now it gets nasty. Look left, Bigeyes, straight along the wall. That's right, a ledge. Yeah, I know. More a mantelpiece than a ledge, but it's strong. I know cos I've been on it before.

And it's all we got now.

Grip the rail, ease one foot off the steps onto the ledge, then the other. Let go of the rail. Shit, Bigeyes, this is worse than I remember. It was bad enough when I wasn't bombed. I got my balance skimming loose again, and the wind's swirling worse than ever.

Stay still, dead still, breathe. Nothing to hold on to now. Just the flat wall against me and nothing to grip. Keep my face to the wall, take another breath, inch myself along, step, step, step. Got to reach the far edge. Got to just . . . reach the far edge.

Step. Step. Step.

Wind's getting worse. Colder, stronger. I want to look down, check if there's grinks watching. But I can't. I got my face close against the wall. And I don't dare shift it.

Step. Step. Step.

Edge of the wall's getting closer. Another ten steps and I'm there. If I can just keep upright, not buck out. Cos I want to. I'm telling you, Bigeyes, I'm close to losing my drift.

But here's the edge.

And here's the next jip. Cos it's not over yet, Bigeyes. That was the fun bit just gone. Gets worse now. Up to the edge, hand round, arm round, inch past onto the other wall. And now, check again. What do you see?

Ledge continues along this wall. And farther along?

Drainpipe cutting through it, up and down. That's right, Bigeyes. We got to reach that. And then we got to climb down. And then . . .

Follow the pipe with your eyes.

Thirty feet down, forty maybe—little guttery thing in the wall. See it? Kind of like a stone basin. Don't ask me what it does. But that's where we put our feet, that's where we launch off. Where to?

Look left. Look down.

Yeah, Bigeyes. Told you this was a whack. We got to jump down onto the top of the Grosvenor Hotel. Don't ask me how far it is. I don't want to think about it. Enough to break a few bones if you hit the roof badly.

But the alternative's a lot worse.

And it is jumpable. There's kids do this kind of thing all the time. I used to be good at it. And this jump's a jink if you know how to do it. If you're into jumping over roofs. Which I was. When I was strong. And desperate.

Only now I'm not strong.

Just desperate.

So I guess it's jump and hope. A chance of safety if I make it. A three- or four-second drop if I don't. Just long enough to say good-bye to sweet Becky before the ground splats out my life.

Let's go.

Down the ledge, steady. Keep up, Bigeyes. Don't dawdle. I'm not doing this on my own. Keep moving. It's when you stop that you freeze in your head. And then you're stuffed. Got to keep moving, keep thinking it's possible.

Cos it is.

I keep telling myself it is. I know I'm blasted. Body's smashed, mind's smashed. But I got to keep telling myself I can do it. I found something to nail that scumbo. Something fear gave me. I need that again.

I need it now.

Or in a couple of short minutes. When I'm standing on that stony lip. I got to find that thing again. The strength, nerve, luck—whatever it is fear grubbed into me last time. I need it back. I need fear to deliver.

Here's the drainpipe. Got to watch things big-time now. Got to hang on good. It's not about standing anymore. That was hard enough. But I need strength for this. Got to grip that thing tight. If it slips out of my arms, I'm falling.

And it's over.

Ease round, one leg, slow. Test the foot against the side, dig the toe in behind the pipe, lock it against the wall. Feels cute but I haven't put any weight on it yet. Breathe, breathe again. I don't like this, Bigeyes. I don't feel safe.

But I got to do it.

Arm round the pipe, tight as I can, ease my body round. I'm clinging on now and I can feel my weight pulling me back. Cling on, tighter, tighter. I'm still there. I haven't fallen. Not yet.

Ease down, other foot digging round the pipe into the wall, then the first foot again, arms still tight. I feel like a baby clutching its mum. And just as weak. But I'm moving down, foot by foot.

Twist my head, check below. I can see the basin thing. Beyond it the sheer drop. And beyond that, a jump away, the flat roof of the Grosvenor Hotel. Move on, down, down. Mustn't hurry. Got to keep my head. Keep my head and I keep my life.

Or my hope anyway.

Yeah, I'll settle for hope.

Here's the stony lip. Rest my foot on it, arms still locked round the drainpipe. I don't want to let the thing go but I got to. I got to make myself turn, face the drop, face the roof. Breathe, breathe again, turn.

Slow.

Let go one hand. Got to or I can't turn. Right arm's still clutching the pipe, left arm's free. I'm half round now, checking my footing on the lip. It's wet and slippery where water from the drain's splattered over it. But I got to trust it. The lip's all I got to stand on now.

And somehow I got to let go my right arm.

Ease it free from the pipe, turn right round. Both arms behind me now, hands clasping the pipe. I never felt so naked in my life. And I've felt naked many times, Bigeyes. You better believe it.

But now's not the time to talk about that.

Now I got to jump.

Only I can't. I'm rigid. I'm stuck on the edge of a wall, looking down at the ground far below me. Only it's so dark I can hardly see it. There's no lights below. It's the side of the hospital. A lane where the delivery vans come in.

But I can't see 'em. Can't see any figures either.

Maybe there's grinks there. Maybe not. I've stopped caring. Cos there's only one thing left now. One way to go. Peer over at the roof of the hotel. Did it always look so far away? I used to jump this for fun.

But it's a long time since I did anything for fun.

Good-bye, Bigeyes.

11 ANOTHER DARKNESS, ANOTHER DEATH.

Another question. What is this place? Cos you know what? I've stopped knowing what lives, what dies. Stopped caring, almost. All that's certain is darkness. And the sound of sirens. And then I get it.

Death's tricked me yet again. Some gobbo, that Death. I hate him. But I'm coming to respect him. And I'll tell you what—he's a trickster. It's all sleight of hand with him. Not with others. The gobbo in the storeroom's dead. No messing. He's not coming back. Same as sweet Becky's dead. And don't ask me how many others.

But me? Me and Death? He's playing with me. He's having a giggle. He likes me not knowing. He leaves me with darkness. And questions. And the sound of sirens again. And then I know.

I'm alive. I'm lying somewhere. The roof of the hotel, that's it. I've been blacko again. But now I'm awake, I'm aching all over, shivering, moaning, weeping stupid little tears out of my stupid little eyes.

And somewhere below I can hear 'em. The wailing of sirens. I know what that means. They've found the gobbo's body. They've found I've gone. Question is: who knows where I am now?

Are you there, Bigeyes? Cos I can't see you. Maybe you've gone. I got my eyes open, haven't I? Shit, they're closed.

Open my eyes. Still dark. Night's fallen over me like a cold kiss. But I can see the sky clear and good. I'm lying on my back, and I'm shivering and crying, and my body's hurting, and I'm looking up at the sky.

And there's stars out.

And a moon. A big, bright, funny-face moon.

God, it's beautiful.

Where are you, Bigeyes? I still can't see you. But it doesn't matter. I can see the moon and the stars. And they're better looking than you are anyway. But now I got you again. You're still there. Like a smelly shirt.

Always clinging on.

Don't know if I'm pleased. Don't know what I think.

Just know I can't stay here watching the sky. If I stay here, there'll be no question marks with Death. No sleight of hand. He'll fold me up and put me in his little bag. But I'll tell you something, Bigeyes. If I had to go tonight, I'd like to go like this.

Looking at the stars. And the funny-face moon.

But I'm not ready to go yet.

I got to move my stump. You too, Bigeyes. We're getting out of here. I made it to the roof. I can't give up now. Not while we still got a chance. But first things first. Check for injuries.

Nothing. Must have landed smart. Don't remember it. Don't remember the jump or the landing. Must have been instinct did it. Don't remember hitting anything bad either. The blacko must have come from exhaustion.

Question is: how much more have I got left?

Roll over onto my side. Aching everywhere but no breaks, not even a sprain. Get up. Get yourself up. Make yourself do it. Up, swaying again. Head's like a fog but the cold's helping like it did before. Got to watch myself, got to keep thinking. Got to keep low. There's grinks all round the streets and the porkers coming will have scattered 'em farther about.

There's no way out of any of the hotel exits. Too close to the hospital. I got to roof-hop a bit more. Just as well the jumps are easier from here. And just as well I know my way. I might even get a good whip on my first plan.

The snug. There's one near here. I told you. If I can just get there without the grinks or porkers clogging me, I can rest up, sort my head, blast out of the city.

Cos there's no staying here now, Bigeyes. City's over for me. She's been good to me. But stay much longer and she'll turn into my grave. I got to get away, somewhere safe, if I can find it. Or if I can't, then . . .

Back to the Beast. Yeah, the Big Beast.

Did I ever tell you about him?

Don't suppose I did. Cos I don't like talking about him. He's a place, Bigeyes. Huge great place. Bigger than the city, way bigger. And he's no gentleman. Least the city's a lady some of the time. The Beast's a gentleman none of the time.

You don't want to know him.

And neither do I. But I'm starting to wonder, you know? If I can't find somewhere else to hide, maybe I just got to go back. I don't want to. The Beast's the last place on earth I want to go.

It's where they first got me. Where they won't be expecting me. Maybe I could take the fight to them. But I'm talking grime now. First I got to stay alive. Got to get through the next five minutes.

The Beast can wait. I'll think about him another time.

On, over the roof, heading east. Keep to the middle. Hotel's a beauty for keeping out of sight. At this point anyway. Only place higher is the hospital and I'm hoping no neb's looking down from the upper floors.

Can't do much about that now anyway. Any luck and there'll be too much fuss over the dead body. But there'll be a police block round this part of the city soon enough. They'll know I can't get far.

So I got to get out quick as I can.

End of the hotel roof. Now the fun starts again. Down the pipe, easy jump to the roof of the bank. Over the tiles, keeping back from the street. On to the edge of the roof, drainpipe down to the next level, another easy jump to the library, and now it stays cute for a bit.

Buildings close together, almost like a terrace. I'm hoping one of the windows'll let me in so I can creep back down to the ground. There's one I know always used to be open. Dodgy catch and rotten timber. It's at the end of the row too. Best place to get out of here.

Clamber on. I'm hurrying now and I got to watch it. Hands and legs are sort of working but they're still not right. They're not feeling their way like they should. Head's still bad, and I'm fighting blacko again. I just want to get warm and curl up.

Even if it means I never wake again.

I got to fight that. I got to want life more than death.

Another roof gone, another, another. Sirens still screaming in the streets. How many porkers have gone past now? I don't know. They're all heading for the hospital. And I'm pushing hard the other way.

If I can just get down to the street, it's five minutes to my snug.

Another roof gone, and another, and here it is. The pizzeria. Only the pizzeria bit's lower down. Top part of the building's offices and storerooms and stuff. No one's ever there this time of night. I'm just hoping nobody's fixed that old window.

If the same nebs are still running the place, we might be lucky.

Over the tiles, round the far side, keep low. Down the drainpipe to the lower roof, along the flat, round the side, down the next pipe. Got to be slickeye now. We're much closer to the street. Just a side lane underneath us but there's nebs wandering up and down.

And they're twitchy now that the porkers have started whopping their sirens.

But here's the window.

And yeah, you beauty—just as rotten as ever. Cling to the drainpipe, check the thing over. Voices from the lane below. Two waiters from the pizzeria, having a cig. Can't move till they're gone. They might hear me shift the window.

Another siren from the street. Gobbos head back to look.

Yank the window, flick the catch. Window opens and I'm in. Close it after me, slip through the room and out to the landing. I know where this leads. I slapped it rough here one time, sleeping among the boxes in one of the storerooms when it got too cold to kip on the roof. Same old landing. Same old stairs.

And I don't have to go near the pizza restaurant.

I can use the back door.

Down the stairs, slow, quiet. Head's still hurting and I'm desperate to lie down. But I can smell my escape. And my little snug just minutes away. Down to the ground floor, wait in the shadows by the entrance to the cellar. Sound of voices in the kitchen. Farther on, the clamor of the restaurant.

Turn from them, past the cellar, out the back door and into the yard. More sirens scream past in the street beyond. But this gate opens onto the lane. Check round it. Dark, empty. No porkers, no grinks.

Nobody.

I'm gone.

12

OKAY, YOU'VE SEEN a couple of the snugs I use at night. And one of my daytime snugs. But they were all empty, right? Well, this is a third type. One where the owner's there too.

Only works with certain places and certain people. I don't like using these snugs. They're risky even if the owner's dimpy in the head. I use 'em only when I'm desperate. Like I am now.

But I should be okay here. The dunny's pretty deaf and she's got a gammy leg. Spends most of her time on the ground floor. Got her bedroom and bathroom down there and everything else she needs.

Proper stingebucket and a mouth like mud. I used to hear her slagging her lodgers when they complained. Wouldn't spend shit on their rooms but you name it, she's got it in hers. Bloody palace downstairs. Cop a glint through her windows and you'll see what I mean.

She's one spitty cow.

Lodgers have all moved out now. So I make use of her attic room when I got nowhere else to go. We got to be quiet though, Bigeyes. Back door and move soft, okay?

There's the house. Big old thing at the end. Light on bottom right, curtains drawn. Got it? That's the lounge. She's probably in there with the television on. Let's go.

Stop by the house, check round. All quiet in the street.

Sleepy place, this. Don't know if that's good or bad. Usually it's good. Right now I'm wary of everything. No sign of anyone watching from the street or the other houses.

No sign of the old dunny.

"You!"

Shit, it's her. Standing in the front door. Never saw her come out, never heard her. What's the matter with me? I don't miss things like that.

"You!" she calls again.

She's looking straight at me.

"What are you hanging around for?"

"I'm not hanging around."

"Yes, you are. You're standing outside my house. And this is a cul-de-sac. It goes nowhere. So what are you hanging around for?"

"I got lost."

"You're not lost. I've seen you here before. Loitering."

I don't believe this, Bigeyes.

"Well?" she says.

I turn away, set off down the road. She calls after me, same bossy voice.

"Help me carry this."

I stop, look round. She's disappeared inside the house but the front door's still open. She comes back, staggering with a big box.

"Take it, for God's sake!" she says.

I hurry back, up to the front door, take the box. Stuffed to the brim with broken crockery and empty plant pots. She gives me an imperious look.

"Put it round the side of the house. By the green garbage can."

I carry it round, put it down, walk back. She's still standing in the doorway. Looks me over like I'm a dronk, then jets another question.

"What have you done to your forehead?"

"Nothing."

"You've got a long cut. Have you been in a fight?"

"I got to go."

"Wait there."

She disappears inside the house, comes back a moment later.

"Lean forward."

I lean forward. She dabs something moist on my forehead. Stings bad.

"Keep still."

She glares at me and goes on dabbing, then presses a big plaster over the wound.

"You need to get that properly seen to." Another imperious look. "I've just done a patch-up job. You should get yourself to the hospital. And keep out of fights."

She takes a step back, looks me up and down again.

"Now clear off."

And she closes the door.

13

BUT I DON'T CLEAR OFF. I can't, Bigeyes. I got no strength left for anywhere else. It's here or nowhere. Check round. No sign of her peering out, or any other nebs watching.

Round the back.

All quiet. Curtains not drawn in the kitchen. Check through the window. See what I mean? Twinky gear. She's not short of money. Check the back door. It's usually un-locked but I keep a nail under that stone in case I have to pick it.

But we're all right. It's unlocked. Ease open, listen cute. Sound of the television from inside the lounge. Pretty sure she's in there. Slip in, close the door. Okay, Bigeyes, listen up.

Simple rules for this snug. We move quick and we move quiet. Got to get past the lounge and upstairs crack-smart. But we'll take some food with us. Apples, pastry, mineral water. That'll do. Let's go.

Down the hall, past the lounge, up the stairs. First floor, stop, listen. Sound of a cough from inside the lounge. Televi-sion still on. Up to the second floor, listen again. All's well. Check round, Bigeyes. Look at the cabinets. My other reason for coming here.

Books.

Cabinets full of 'em. Downstairs, both landings, see? She's

got some good 'uns too. Worth the risk sometimes just to come here and read.

Into the upstairs bathroom. Turn the tap on, quiet. Splash my face, wash my hands, look up. I've been putting this moment off, Bigeyes. And it's worse than I thought.

Not the wound. Dunny's covered that pretty good with the plaster. And just as well. Must look a globby sight after shunting all that blood, never mind the other stuff Dig's knife ripped up.

No, it's my face.

I'm scared of my face.

I told you before about me and mirrors. I got to check my face every snug I go to. Make sure it's not turned so bad I can't bear to look at it. I'm dreading the day that happens. Only now I'm not seeing my face at all.

I'm seeing that gobbo's face. The one lying dead in the storeroom. And now I'm looking at me. Like I'm dead too. I got to rest. Got to eat and drink and sleep. I'll think better when I've done all that. I'll be able to fight again. Live again. Get away.

Out of the bathroom, listen again. Just the television like before. Up the last set of stairs to the attic room. Books here too, see? Cabinets outside the room, either side of the door.

Romeo and Juliet.

Read that last time I was here. Book's still in the same place on the shelf.

Oliver Twist.

Read that too. Only not here.

Push open the door.

Nothing's changed. Same grubby hole. But it's got a bed. And the bed's got a mattress and a pillow. I'm aching to lie down now. But I got to eat first. Slump on the bed, grab the pastry, stuff it down. Same with the apples. Drink the mineral water.

Lie back. Try and sleep. Only I don't.

I can't.

I want to sleep so bad, Bigeyes. I want to forget, just for a bit. But I can't. Can't sleep, can't forget. And you know what? Sometimes even when I sleep, I don't forget. The pictures come to me in dreams.

The faces, the things I've done.

Do you reckon Scumbo gets that? Do his pictures follow him around? Does he ever get a moment—one tiny little moment—when he cares? I don't suppose so. He's like all the other grinks. One life on the outside, another life on the inside. He's probably got a wife somewhere who makes jam and thinks he's an insurance salesman.

I've seen too many like him. He's one of the old crowd. Nobody high up. Higher than Paddy's dregs, but nowhere near the top. He'll have known his pay-daddy but nobody else. Not the spikes who are pulling his strings.

There's a lot worse than him coming.

So why do my pictures follow me around? And why's everything changed? If I couldn't kill Scumbo or Paddy, how come I killed all the others? And how come I care? That's what haunts me now, Bigeyes. How come I care?

Close my eyes.

Still can't sleep. Maybe I should read. That usually settles my head, except when the flashbacks are hitting too bad. But I need to sleep, need to rest. Cos tomorrow I got to run again, got to be strong enough to break free.

If I read, I won't sleep.

And anyway, I know the dunny's books too well. She doesn't keep the kind of stories I want right now. Like the one I read last year. Can't remember what it's called. Found it in a snug on the south side. It was a children's book with these wispy pictures. About a boy who stows away on a ship.

How dimpy is that, Bigeyes? I'm terrified of water but I love sea stories.

Anyway, he stows away on this ship, gets found out, and they make him work his passage. But he's a good lad and he makes friends with the captain. And then this big storm blows up, and the crew put off in the boats cos the ship's going to sink, but they forget to take the boy with 'em.

But it's okay, Bigeyes. You know why? Cos the captain's stayed behind, so the boy's not on his own. He doesn't feel lonely. He's got a friend with him, a big, strong friend, who's going to look after him whatever happens. Even if they drown, he's got a friend with him.

But they don't drown.

The lifeboat gets out in the nick of time and takes 'em back to the shore.

I'm so tired, Bigeyes. Tired of running, tired of being on my own, tired of being scared. Like I'm on a sinking ship too, only I got no captain to look after me. And no lifeboat coming to take me home.

Just this.

An attic room in someone else's house.

But sleep's coming. Least I got that now. I can feel it. A beautiful, warm darkness. It folds round me. I'm dying in my head, Bigeyes. I'm blasted. I just want to dive deep and stay safe for a bit.

And I do. For a few sweet hours.

Till I wake again, trembling. It's dark, it's cold. The house is still.

But there's footsteps on the stairs.

14

SLIP OFF THE BED, knife open, ear to the door.

It's not the dunny.

It's grinks.

Don't ask me how I know.

Footsteps have stopped, halfway up the last flight of stairs. Hard to tell how many nebs. Definitely more than one. They're listening. Listening for me. Like I'm listening for them.

Back to the window, quiet, quick. Keep to the side, check out. Shadows moving round the back door. Two, three, four. There'll be more outside the front of the house.

And there's two at least on the stairs.

Back to the door, listen cute. Still silence. Got to wait. Got to hold back. They might just go. But I don't think so. They've come up this far. They'll check the attic room. They've checked the others. They'll check this one too. They wouldn't be here at all if someone hadn't seen me.

They'll come on. I know they will. But I got to wait. Just in case.

Still the silence. It feels like a mist. Buzz my eyes round the room. Nowhere to hide in here. Bad idea anyway. It's a simple choice now. Fight or die. Moment the footsteps start again, I'll know. If they head down the stairs, I stay quiet. Up the stairs and I blow. They start.

Up the stairs.

I'm out the door, knife up.

Two gobbos near the top. Never seen 'em before. They stop, fix me. Smooth types, like Scumbo, like Paddy. Only more dangerous.

"How you doing, kid?" says one. "We heard you lost your bottle."

"I just found it again. Looking at you dungpots."

He smirks back at me.

"I don't think so. That's two in a row you've let go. First Paddy, then—"

"He got away, did he?"

"Oh, yeah. He got away."

"How's his thumb? How's his little finger?"

"Healing nicely." Gobbo gives me a wink. "Don't know why you're holding that knife. Since you lost the guts to use it. Might as well come with us, kid. Breaking fingers and thumbs won't get you very far here."

"Piss off!"

"Time to come home," he mocks. "Time to meet some old friends."

They start up the stairs. I reach out, grab some books and fling 'em. William Shakespeare and Charles Dickens clock 'em in the face. I pull the cabinet, pull again. It lurches, tips, falls. And now it's thundering toward 'em.

Knocks both gobbos back down the stairs. I'm down after 'em. They're floundering on the landing but they're struggling back up. Jump over 'em, down the next flight of stairs to the first floor. Voices behind me, the gobbos yelling. Sound of footsteps running from the street. More yelling behind me. I'm on the next flight now, jumping down to the hall.

Dunny's lying dead at the bottom of the stairs.

Over her and off toward the drawing room. No point going for the front door. That's the way they'll come in. Door crashes open right that moment. Two gobbos burst through, followed by two more. Sound of footsteps from the back door.

Into the drawing room, slam the door, race to the window. I'm praying it's not stiff. Catch flicks back. Yank the window open, clamber out. Narrow path round the side of the house, fence straight in front of me.

I jump onto it and start to climb.

A hand grabs me from behind. Some gobbo's caught me from the drawing room window. Whip back with the knife, gash him in the face. He gives a roar and lets go. More gobbos crowd round the window. One starts to edge through.

But I'm up halfway over the fence now. Slip down the other side, stumble into next door's garden. I'm screaming now, top of my voice.

"Police! Call the police!"

Lights go on inside the house. I run over to the pond, pick up a garden gnome, fling it at the greenhouse. It crashes through like a bomb. Window opens in the house and a gobbo roars down.

"Hoy!"

"Police!" I shout. "Police!"

"Who's down there? What going on?"

I don't answer. I'm stumbling through flower beds toward the next garden. Gobbo in the window goes on bellowing but there's no sign of the grinks. I reach the opposite fence, climb over. Guy's still bawling into the night and there's lights on all over his house. Run down to the bottom of the next garden.

Stop, think, just for a second. Got to crank my head. Got to work out which way to go. Can't just blunder about. The grinks'll have grouped and they're still close. They'll hang back cos of the porkers coming but they'll call more grinks and flood the area.

They know where I am now. And they know I'm weak.

They're right. I got no strength to spare. Fear did it again, got me away, but it won't keep me running forever. I got to go to ground somehow. Got to stay safe through the night. And somehow . . .

Got to break free.

I'm so scared, Bigeyes.

Check round again. Still no grinks in sight but they'll be looking for ways to get past the houses into the gardens. They know I'm somewhere on this side. Harder to reach me with the nebs waking up but that won't stop 'em. Lights going on in all the houses now. I got to wig it fast as I can. Which way?

There's no good place now, no easy snug. Dunny's was the only one near enough. I feel bad about her, Bigeyes. I didn't like her but I didn't want her dead. And they stiffed her cos of me. But I can't think about that now. I can hear voices from the houses.

Check round the fence. I know what's on the other side. Scrubby ground down to the railway line, building site beyond that, and then the houses start again. Let's get moving. Over the fence, down the other side, check for sounds.

No more voices but the distant wail of sirens.

Getting closer.

Move on. Got to move on. If I stop, I'm dead. I don't just mean the grinks. I mean the cold. It's fifty-fifty now. That's how it is. No messing, Bigeyes. This could be it.

Down the hill. Watch the ground. It's uneven. You can turn an ankle easy as wink. And we got enough problems without that as well. There's the railway line. Old signalman's hut over to the right. Can't shelter there. It's the first place they'll look. Got to go farther. Think of somewhere they won't try.

Won't be easy.

They'll try everywhere.

Edge down the bank, check round, cross over the rails, up the other side, walk on. Getting colder, Bigeyes. I don't like this. It was bad enough before but now it's getting worse. Can't be more than two in the morning and it'll be a good few hours before it gets warmer.

If it does.

Walk on, over the waste ground. I've thought of somewhere, Bigeyes, somewhere we can rest. And it's close. But it's bad, really bad. It won't be warm, it probably won't be safe. It's not a place to die in. But what choice have we got now?

See the fence round the building site? Walk up, stop outside, peer through. Looks like a bomb site, yeah? They're supposed to be putting up a shopping complex. Lots of nice warm buildings—only they're not here yet. So we'll make do with a pipe.

Yeah, I know.

But there's nowhere else I can get to now. We got to slap it like duffs. If I can just get the strength for this last climb.

Breathe slow, check round. Got to be careful even here. They got a night watchman somewhere.

But he's not very hardworking.

No sign of him. No sign of dogs.

Or grinks.

Means nothing. But we got to give it a go.

Up the fence, hand over hand. Least it's an easy climb. Drop down the other side, scramble round the perimeter, down into the ditch on the right. You're wondering how I know my way, right? I told you once before, Bigeyes.

I watch. I remember.

And now I'm glad. Cos this is our place for the rest of the night. And it's free. Down to the bottom of the ditch, into the pipe, curl up in the darkness, close my eyes. And now there's a new choice.

Sleep or die. Or maybe both.

And you know what, Bigeyes?

I don't much care now which one I get.

15

ONLY I'M LYING. I do care. I can't sleep, Bigeyes. And right now I can't die either. Maybe it'll come in an hour or so. Right now all I can do is shiver. And think. And cry.

Why'm I'm crying? Eh? Why? Effing bloody tears. Who does that help? Not me. Not anybody else. They won't make me live. They won't make me die. They won't bring sweet Becky back.

Or that spitty old dunny lying at the foot of her staircase. Or the gobbo in the hospital storeroom. Won't make his missus feel better. Or his family. Or the others. Yeah, there's others I could tell you about. I can see all their faces.

I'm still holding the knife, see?

Scumbo's little toy.

And here's what I hate. I've been holding it all this time. But I haven't noticed. Like you don't notice you got hands and feet. Not unless you look for 'em special. Most of the time you just know you got 'em. You take 'em for granted.

Like this knife.

I just take it for granted. I remember the attic room, the footsteps on the stairs. I remember slipping off the bed, and there's the knife ready in my hand. But I don't remember pulling it out of my pocket. I don't remember flicking it open.

Maybe it was already open.

Maybe I was already holding it.

I don't remember, Bigeyes. That's the crack of it. The knife was just there. Like my hands and feet are just there. And now here it is again. Blade open. Tight in my grip.

Look around you, Bigeyes. This is our world now. Darkness, cold, danger. A ditch of sand and sludge. A pipe. A knife that won't die. And tears. It's like I'm made of tears.

I can't get my head round that. Maybe it's just cos I'm ill. Cos I know I'm dying. Still shivering too. I won't get any sleep tonight. Might just as well get used to that. I'm going to shiver my way into Death's black heart.

And then?

God knows. If there is a God. I don't much care, you know?

Tell you why. Cos he shoved me on Day One. That's when the trouble started. Day bloody One. I saw a bit of that picture when I was spooking my head in the ambulance. Or felt it anyway.

My mum and dad—whoever they were—took one look at me and said no. They might just as well have put me here.

In this pipe.

Only they put me in another kind of pipe. And left me. How do I know? Cos I remember the nebs who found me. And what they told me. And what they did. And that's when I knew there can't be a God.

Not one who loves me anyway.

If there is, he's busy somewhere else.

Anyway, it's too late now. I'm shivering my life away and I'm crying and I just want it to be over. But now it's all starting again. Cos I can see a shadow moving on the other side of the ditch.

Can't I even die in peace?

Hard to know what to do. Wriggle to the opening and check out if it's danger or wriggle farther in and keep out of sight. Best to keep out of sight, but if it's grinks and they look in, I'm plugged.

Got to check it out.

Knife's still tight in my fist, see? Same again. It's just there. I don't have to think about it. It's just there. Anyway . . .

Wriggle toward the opening, peer out.

It's a gobbo, middle-aged. And I know him.

Well, just. He's a muffin anyway. Sort of a deadhead duff who hangs around refuse dumps. I've seen him a few times. He's no trouble. Long as he's not looking for conversation. That could bring the grinks.

Cos they're still close.

I can feel it.

Christ, he's seen me. He's coming over.

Big brute of a guy, harmless but thick. I got to get rid of him. He lumbers over, stops outside the pipe, swaying like he's drunk. But he always does that. He's staring down at me, eyes wide, mouth chewing air.

"Get lost," I say.

He doesn't move, just stands there, gawping, like he doesn't know what to do.

"Clear off," I say.

He goes on staring, scratches his head, gives a sneeze.

"Cold," he says suddenly.

"Yeah, it's cold. Now beat it."

I gesture with the knife.

He still doesn't go. What's wrong with this guy? I got nothing against him but I want him gone. He scratches his head again, shrugs.

"Cold," he murmurs. "It's . . ."

He doesn't finish, just turns and slopes off round to the right. There's more pipes that way. He's probably looking for one of those. Stick my head out to make sure he's gone.

Yeah, he's wigged it. Let's hope the grinks leave him alone.

And us.

I feel bad about shoving him off. He meant no harm. But it's too dangerous having him around. And anyway, I got no strength for talk. No taste either. If I'm going to die, I don't want the likes of him watching.

I want to be on my own.

Roll over onto my back, peer up.

Hey, Bigeyes, check that out. Night sky, just like it was before. Maybe I should stay like this with my head out of the pipe, take a risk. I might get seen but I might not.

And I wanted to die looking up at the stars. And the funny-face moon.

I'll take a risk. Yeah, why not?

Jesus, Bigeyes, it's crazy up there. All that darkness and all that light. There's Orion, see? I recognize it. There was this book in one of my snugs about astronomy. Written by some professor gobbo.

He said stars are like people. They're born, they grow up, they get old, and they die. The silvery bright ones are the young stars. The reddy orange ones are the old'uns. And they're billions and billions and billions of miles away. There's not enough noughts on the calculator to say how far away they are.

And our planet's nothing.

I'm telling you, Bigeyes, it's a speck of nothing. If it blows up tomorrow, the universe won't even notice. Time and space and all this stuff'll just go on like we never existed.

Cos we don't matter. We're nothing, you and me. Look up, Bigeyes. Take it all in. We're just hopes and dreams. And then some more.

As for the stars . . .

I'll tell you something else that gobbo said in his book. He said some of the stars are dead before their light even gets here. That's right, Bigeyes. Some of those lights come from ghosts.

I could be looking at people up there.

And maybe I am.

Some alive, some dead.

All winking in the darkness. Cos the dead don't go. I'm telling you, Bigeyes, they don't go. You could kill everyone in the world and they'll just go on winking in the darkness. Your darkness. Till you're dead too. And then all the lights go out.

As for the moon . . .

That's just a dead thing too.

But at least its light comes quicker. And right now it's brightening the blade of Scumbo's knife. Hold it up. Looks almost pretty in my hand.

Fold it up, put it away.

Close my eyes.

I've seen enough of the night sky. I'll keep the stars in my head, and the moon, and the knife. And the winking lights of the nebs who've died.

16

DAWN. I'M SHIVERING, but I've slept. And I'm still alive. Why'm I still alive? Something's happened. I got a coat draped over me.

Stiffen, check round. My head's still out of the pipe, looking up. Rest of me's huddled into a ball, frozen up. Knife's clutched in my hand, blade open. Don't remember pulling it out again. And the coat . . .

It's that gobbo's coat. The duff's. I recognize it. His heavy old coat. Squirm out of the pipe, check round. Got a mixture of feelings choking me up. Scared cos I didn't feel him come close, throw it over me.

That freaks me, Bigeyes. Cos I always know when someone's creeping up. Even when I'm asleep. That's how I've stayed alive. Only this time, when I was freezing and scared and restless, the duff comes right up, nails this on me and I never wake up.

And here's the other feeling that's choking me up.

Cos no one's ever done that to me before. Slipped me a coat. Why should they? Why should he? I said I know him, sort of. But only to nod. Not like I'd help him. Not like he'd help me. I thought. 'Specially after I was rude to him.

I'm choked up. I'm telling you.

He might even have saved my life with this coat.

But I can't think about that now. I got to decide what to do. We can't stay here. We got to be well gone before the site crew turn up. Question is: where to go? I didn't expect to be alive this morning. Trouble is I'm still weak. I got no energy. Well, not much.

And I'm still shivering.

It's more dangerous than yesterday. Way more. First up, no darkness to hide in. Second, there's everybody looking for us now. Grinks obviously but porkers too, and every neb and his dog who's heard the news. Which is most of the city. It'll be worse than ever now that there's been more murders.

Everyone's going to be grilling for me.

So where? I guess it's a simple choice now. I told you I can't stay in the city. She's been good to me but her time's over. So it's either wig it and play dead somewhere else. Or go back to the Big Beast.

And fight 'em where they don't expect it.

Don't like either choice, Bigeyes. Not when I'm blasted like this. Gut tells me wig it. Find somewhere else. It's got to be still possible. There's other cities, other places to play dead. It'll take time to do my watching, find my new snugs. But I did it before. I can do it again. If I can just stay alive. And get away.

Or there's the Beast.

And that decides it. No contest really. I can't face the Beast. Not in this state. Not in any state probably. So it's wig it out of the city. Get through this day, stay alive, stay out of sight, slip away when darkness comes.

Start again somewhere else.

Far away.

There's got to be places just as good as this city. Big places full of snugs. Places where I can be safe. Even if I can't be forgotten. Cos that's the problem, Bigeyes. That's why I got it wrong before. Part of me thought if I play dead long enough, they'll forget about me. Let me slip away. And the past won't matter. Only I was bung-stupid. Should have known better.

The spikes don't forget.

So the grinks keep coming. They'll always keep coming. So my next place has got to be better than this one. But that's looking too far ahead. Right now we got the biggest problem of all. Getting through to tonight.

I got a plan.

Or let's say an idea. All depends on how things go. If I can walk for starters. And not get recognized. This duff's coat'll help a bit. It's got a hood. Got to be careful though. Dodgy walking with a hood up when it's not raining. Porkers come sniffing straightaway.

So it's a bit of a bum gripe. Hood down and I'm dung. Hood up and I look suspicious. But there's nothing much I can do about that. Have to chance it. See what's round me and do what feels best.

Let's go.

Pull the coat on proper, do up the buttons. Feels warmer right off, but I'm still shivering. Got to get moving and keep moving. Out of the ditch, check round. All still, apart from a cat climbing on the digger. No sign of the night watchman or any grinks.

But I don't feel right. There's too many of 'em to lose now. And they're still close. I can feel it. Over to the fence, check again. Something moving in the bushes on the other side, something black. A dog sniffing round. Makes me think of Buffy for a moment. But this one's not interested in me.

I start to climb. Dog turns its head, fixes me. I'm halfway up the fence.

Don't bark, doggy.

And don't come over.

He doesn't do either. Just looks a bit more, then lopes off. I'm down the other side of the fence, checking round again. Nothing moving anywhere. Even the dog's disappeared.

Right, Bigeyes. Before the world wakes up.

Round the outside of the fence, off toward the estate. I don't come this way much. No decent snugs to speak of, nothing much to nick. But there is something I want. If I can just get there. But first things first.

Food.

I'm desperate for food.

Head's thumping now and I'm aching all over. Still shivering, still bombed out. And I'm crying again. Can't stop myself. Something about that duff and his coat. I'm still holding the knife too.

Jesus, Bigeyes. What is it about this thing?

I've been carrying it open since I crawled out of the pipe. Fold it up, put it in the coat pocket. Feels big and heavy, even though it's light. I'm going to try and forget about it. For a bit anyway. And I suppose I don't need to worry. If there's grinks, it'll find my hand without me looking.

Like it always does.

Walk on, hood down. But I'm checking round me dead cute. Still quiet everywhere. No nebs to be seen yet. Robin perched on the fencepost farther down. Takes no notice of me. Walk past and on down the track toward the children's playground. Through the swings and round to the exit.

Check again.

First of the streets, but all's still.

Hood up even so. It's risky now. Got to keep my head

down, face hidden. Walk slow, side of the road. Sound of a car behind me. Let's hope it's nobody. No porkers or grinks anyway.

Just a van, doesn't stop.

Walk on, cut right round the back of the garage, past the roundabout, over the bridge, round the parade of shops. And there's the supermarket at the end. Still quiet but we got to watch out. There's nebs who like looking out of windows. And there's cameras.

But I can't be worrying too much now. I got to find something to eat.

This probably won't work. It's usually only certain times when you get stuff. And you got to be quick or the regular duffs get in first. Not expecting much this time of the morning. And if there is anything, it might not be any good. But we'll try anyway.

Round the back to the Dumpsters. Open the first. Nothing I can use. Same with the next, same with the next. Last one's got a packet of bread rolls, well past the sell-by. Grab it and go. Out to the street, check again. Baker shop farther down's got the door open. I can smell the bread even from here. Edge down, stop by the door.

But I can't go in. There's nebs walking down the street toward me. Students by the look of 'em, like they're coming back from an all-night party. I can't cream anything from the baker's till they've gone. They walk past, don't even notice me.

Watch 'em go, then check through the baker's door. But it's no good. There's two gobbos in there, working the ovens. Cross the road, away from the shops, down into the park, slump on the first bench. And I'm into the bread rolls.

Christ, they taste good. I don't care if they're old. I'm just stuffing 'em down. And now up and off. Cos this is the next stage, Bigeyes. Yeah, I know. Dronky breakfast, but there's no time to look for more. We got to shift to the next place. Grab what we can for the journey. And then hide again till dark.

Let's move.

17

BUT IT'S GETTING HARDER. Moving, I mean. Those rolls made no difference. Tasted good cos I'm hungry but no energy in 'em. Not much in me either. I feel like I'm dragging myself. But we got to keep going.

Out of the park and down Kensall Lane. Hood up, head down. But check round you, Bigeyes. We're on the north side of the city here and it's a mean stash. Run-down estates, houses guttered up. No one but drug pushers burning dosh round here.

There's factories down that way but not many. It's mostly pubs and corner shops, and gangs on the streets. Trixi's crew used to come here sometimes. Don't think the other trolls liked it much but she did. She liked to mix it with other dregs when she ran out of people to fight round her own patch.

I got to watch my back here. Cos everyone's going to be twitchy about the murders. And there's gangs on the streets who'll know about Slicky. And one or two who'll recognize me.

Cut left, down toward the primary school. Got to keep moving while the streets are quiet. There's only one thing I ever come here for and you'll soon see what that is. Cos we're going to need it if we get away.

That's right, Bigeyes. We're talking *if*. Cos I'll tell you something—we're in deep grime. The porkers and grinks'll be watching every road out of the city. So I can't take any of the usual routes. I got to play it cute. I thought of a way out but it's risky. And with so many nebs watching, it's no dead smash we'll get away.

But we got to try. Only here's trouble already. Police car nosing down the next street. Just caught a glimpse. Don't think they've seen us yet but if they turn down our street, we're split. Check round. Primary school's nearest.

Over the wall and into the playground, down past the office, round the back to the prefabs. Crouch, wait. Sound of an engine, pulling up in the street we just left. Peep round the side of the nearest classroom.

A car but it's not the porkers. It's another car. Big, black, shiny. All I can see's the hood. But I don't like the look of it. Creep round the back of the prefab, check behind me. No sign of anyone coming. But they are. Car's not there for no reason.

Run to the wall at the far end of the school, climb over it. Front garden of someone's house. Curtains drawn, no sounds inside. Round the side of the building, check behind.

Two gobbos checking round the prefabs. One of 'em's the hairy grunt. The fat man who killed Mary's dog. I recognize the other one too. Lenny, that was his name. One of Paddy's slugs. They're looking my way now.

Don't think they've seen me. But they must have before. And they'll have guessed I'm still close. Lenny's on his mobile now. I got to shift—and quick. Round the side of the wall, into the back garden. Row of gardens stretching away to the right. Houses still sleepy, thank God. I'm just hoping no one's looking out.

Down the garden to the fence, over that, and I'm into an

alleyway running along the bottom. Breathing hard now. Can't keep going like this much longer and I'm still nowhere near where I got to go.

Move. Got to move, no matter what. I can feel the grinks getting closer. I don't have to see 'em. I can feel 'em. I always could. End of the alleyway, cross the road, down the next alleyway. End of that, turn right, past The Jolly Abbot, past the football ground, into the next estate.

Bike in the front garden. Pull it over, jump on, ride, ride.

A mile gone. More estates. No sign of grinks or porkers. But they're still close. I know it. And the world's waking up quick. I can hear voices in the houses, radios, TVs. It's like the dawn chorus of the city. Only there's no birds singing. You don't hear birds in the city. Just nebs switching on their stumpy lives.

And now there's cars moving too.

Early risers, nebs off to work, off to wherever. I'm keeping on the estate, crossing the quiet lanes. But I can see the main road through the gaps, see the big stuff moving. I don't need to be told where the grinks are. I can smell 'em. Police cars too, rumbling up and down. And now the thing I feared most, and earlier than I expected.

Copters.

Two of 'em, well up in the sky, but they're over this part of the city.

Dump the bike, creep up to the wall of the nearest house. The copters are getting closer and the sound's going to bring nebs out of their houses to check what's going on. Front door opens and a crusty old gobbo trigs down to his front gate. Guy next door does the same.

"Bloody things," says Crusty. "This time of the morning."

"They're probably looking for that boy," says the other guy.

It's too good a chance to miss. Round the side of the house, check the back door. It's unlocked. Slip inside Crusty's house. I'm praying he hasn't got a missus. All quiet inside and the gobbo's still by the gate. I can see him through the front door.

Two things I want.

Food and shelter till the copters have gone.

Kitchen first. Apples, oranges, pie in the fridge. Shit, Crusty's coming back. Close the fridge, stuff the food in my pockets, hurry down the hall, into the coat cupboard. Close it almost shut. Mustn't let it click.

Sound of Crusty coming in, front door closing. Copter engines loud overhead. If they've seen me breaking in, I'm plugged. And they might have. They might well have.

But the engines fade away.

Radio goes on in the kitchen.

"The headlines. Police are still looking for a boy aged about fourteen following two new murders in the city. One took place at Central Hospital, where the boy was being treated as a patient. The other was an elderly lady strangled in her home in the Heathside area of the city. The boy was also seen close to the site of this murder. Police are warning the public not to approach the boy, who was last seen wearing—"

Radio goes off. Crusty gives a hacking cough. Sound of footsteps past the coat cupboard and up the stairs. Wait a second, then out into the hall and down to the back door. Looks clear outside but I got to be careful. Open the back door, down to the fence at the bottom of the garden, start to climb.

"You! What are you doing?"

It's Crusty. He's leaning out of the bathroom window, toothbrush in one hand, paste round his mouth.

"What are you doing?"

Another window opens, next door. It's the guy he was speaking to by the gate.

"Everything all right, Mr. Lomax?"

"It's that boy! I recognize him from the description!"

Both gobbos stare at me. I drop over the fence and down the other side. Only now there's no alleyway to hide in. This is the main road and it's packed with cars.

I'm running.

18

BUT IT'S LIKE in a bad dream. When your legs move but you don't move with 'em. You're trying to run but you just flounder and float. I'm starting to panic. It's like there's eyes everywhere now, watching from cars, windows, sidewalks. And here's the copters whirring back.

Into the underpass, through to the other side of the road, down to the shops, left into Castle Mews. Boy delivering papers to the house at the end. He's halfway up the path, bike outside the gate. I jump on and ride. No shout from behind me. He hasn't seen yet.

And now I'm round the corner, pedaling hard. I got a mile to go, Bigeyes. That's all. If I can just get there without being seen. Copters are still up there but they've moved over to the left, like they missed me first time. Up onto the sidewalk.

Got to keep close to the houses, not just cos of the copters and the grinks but the gangs. I told you. It's a rough patch, this. Trixi's old spitting ground. There's bad shit round here. And here's two straight up. Shaven-head dronks, blocking the way. Sixteen, seventeen, mean-looking dingos. I've seen 'em before.

And they've seen me.

"It's Slicky!" calls one.

I'm off the sidewalk but suddenly there's four more. They spread out across the road. I brake, swerve the bike round, pedal back the way I came. Footsteps pounding behind me but I got a head start and I'm pulling away.

"Slicky!" they jeer. "Slicky! Slicky!"

Round the corner, into the next street, ride on. I'm so tired, Bigeyes, so bloody tired. I just want to fall down, sleep, rest, die, whatever. But I can't. I got to get there, got to get away. Got to keep believing I can make it, somehow. Right at the end of the road, on down the next street, right again.

Check round. I'm pretty sure I've skirted the dronks. Got to hope so anyway. Left at the end of the road. All clear. Another half a mile, on, on, on. And now stop, take a breath, think. Okay, Bigeyes, look ahead. Little cluster of houses, then a park with some trees.

We're almost there.

Dump the bike behind the wall.

Yeah, I know. Seems like a dimpy idea. But I'm too easy to see out here. I got to get off the road and I got to do it now. Got to make sure no one sees me from here on. Check round, climb over the wall, walk alongside the road.

Keep low, Bigeyes, and listen for cars. We got to stay out of sight if anything comes along. It's a quiet road, this one, but not that quiet. So listen and keep listening. Here comes something. An engine, behind us.

Duck below the wall. I want to look, see who it is, but I don't dare. Got to wait, got to be patient. Car draws closer. Up in the sky I can see the copters circling. They're still some way off but that means nothing. Who knows how far those nebs can see?

They could be watching me right this moment.

Car draws nearer, slows down. I crouch lower, ready to run. Knife's out already, bright in my hand. Car stops, close by. Sound of a door opening, then a laugh, a gobbo's laugh. And a sound I know. Someone's peeing over the wall.

Just misses me.

Another laugh, door closes, car drives on. I walk on, listening cute. Here's the houses. Got to take this one smart. Cut round the back toward the allotments. They got high fences at the bottom of the gardens and I'm hoping no one'll see me from the houses.

Up to the first, check round. No sign of anyone but a sound of kids playing in one of the gardens. Creep on past, slip down to the allotments, cut over, out the other side, check back. Nobody watching from the top windows. Leave the houses behind, push on toward the park.

I'll tell you something, Bigeyes, I'm looking at those trees now and I'm dreaming. They're like a sanctuary. If we can just get there without being seen, we got a chance.

Shit, another engine. Behind us, like the last one.

Only this is bigger. I'm guessing it's a van, and it's slowing down too. Duck below the wall again, crouch, wait. Something tells me this isn't someone coming for a pee. Draws closer, moving slow, then rolls on past and stops, just ahead, engine ticking over.

Doesn't feel like normal grinks. Can't explain why. But it's trouble.

Don't ask me how I know.

Engine revs up, van moves on, sound fades away. Peep over the wall. No sign of danger, just the park and the trees beckoning. Come on, Bigeyes, this is it. Copters have pulled back, no cars on the road, no nebs watching. We won't get a better chance.

Into the park, into the trees.

At last.

Okay, stick with me, close. Cut right, through the little copse into the alders. We stay on this side of the park. The trees are thicker here. We got to be careful, Bigeyes. There's a lawn over to the left with a pond and a soccer field. We got to keep away from all that in case there's kids playing. So stay in the trees.

Walk on, walk on. Just a short stretch now. Okay, stop.

Hide behind the oak, peer round. See the church down in the dip? Battered old thing with a scruffy little graveyard? Right, now bring your eyes back and look straight in front of you. Little patch of ground. You could almost walk through it and not notice what it is.

But it's not just any patch of ground, Bigeyes.

It's the overflow graveyard.

And not a very popular one. There's only a few stiffos in here. But that's okay, cos one of 'em's a friend of ours. Come on. Over to the far corner, under the spread of the willow. Don't know much about the gobbo buried here. John somebody. That's all I can read.

And no one else seems to care.

He's never got any flowers or anything. But he's got something of ours. Behind the gravestone, the loose rock. Only it doesn't look loose, right? Well, it is. Check around, make sure no one's watching. I don't normally do this in daylight. I come at night, for obvious reasons. But I got no choice now.

Pull up the rock, reach down.

You guessed it.

A bag of goodies. Money first. Quick count. Yep, it's all there. Twelve and a half grand. And some silver. Don't know what I put the coins in for. Yeah, I know. You're wondering how many of these little safes I got.

Loads, Bigeyes. I'm telling you, I got loads, all round the city. And there's not just money in 'em. There's other stuff. Check this.

One diamond. That's all. But he's a big'un. Look at him. Feast on that, Bigeyes. I got more stashed, but this beauty's worth more than all the others put together. And I'll tell you something. There's somebody out there wants him back very badly. And all the other things I've taken.

He wants me back too.

Very badly.

But we won't talk about that now. Pocket the money, diamond back in the hole, wedge down the rock. And now we got to get to our hiding place. Only—

Shit! Freeze!

Voices.

They're close, they're in the trees. Back from the gravestone, check round. No sign of anyone but there's footsteps nearby, and voices again. And suddenly I'm tensed up. Cos I know 'em.

It's the trolls from Trixi's gang.

I can hear Sash, and Tammy, and Xen, and Kat. There's no way they're not looking for me. Maybe that was them in the van. I thought they'd had enough fun with me but I guess I was wrong. God knows how they found me. Maybe they got a message from those dronks.

They're coming this way. Scramble down to the church. If I can just slip round the back, I can maybe get away. Up to the gate, check back. I can see some of the trolls now, moving through the trees. Don't think they've snagged me.

Crouch low, round the back of the church, slump to the ground.

Wait.

Silence. A long one. I hate it. Stare out over the field. There's the lane we got to take out of here. If we can just get there. Can't risk it yet. I'll be easy meat if I cut across the field now. Got to wait. Got to be patient. And hope they go away.

Only they don't.

I can hear footsteps again. Other side of the wall, moving round the church. In a few seconds somebody's going to appear and see me. Footsteps draw closer. They sound strangely quiet, strangely okay. I don't know why that is. A figure appears round the corner of the church. Stands there, looking down at me. And I find I got tears in my eyes. Stupid effing tears.

Cos it's Jaz.

Little Jaz.

19

She's just standing there, looking at me. And I'm looking back. Only I can hardly see her. I got my eyes flooded. I try to wipe 'em. But I can't move my hand. It's like I'm frozen.

Can't think, can't speak, can't move.

Eyes clear a bit. She's still there. I want her to speak. I want her to tell me it's okay. Cos last time I saw her she was terrified of me. Only now it's the other way round. I'm terrified of her. A three-year-old kid. I manage to speak.

"Jaz, it's me, baby."

She comes forward, slow, still watching my face. Suddenly realize I'm holding the knife. I've been holding it all this time, blade open, pointing at her. She doesn't seem to bother about it. She just comes forward.

"It's me, baby," I say.

She stops, just out of reach. I lower the knife, let it slip to the ground. She glances at it, back at me. Doesn't speak. I want her to speak, Bigeyes. I want her to speak so bad. I want her to tell me it's all right.

"I'll never scare you again," I whisper.

Voice calls out, somewhere round the side of the wall. Guy's voice.

"Jaz!"

She holds my eyes a bit longer, then turns and walks back

toward the corner of the church. Guy's voice calls again, closer.

"Jaz!"

She reaches the corner, stops, glances back. I reach up and wipe my eyes. She disappears round the side of the church. Sound of more voices in the churchyard, some of the trolls.

"Where you been, Jaz?"

"We lost you."

"Don't run off, okay?"

No answer from the little kid.

I scramble up, inch over to the edge of the wall, peep round. Six figures moving off. Jaz, Sash, Tammy, Xen, Kat, and then the guy. I recognize him straight off.

Riff.

The slimy. The guy who followed us down the lane that time, gave us away to Paddy and his dregs. He turns suddenly. I hold still. More dangerous to pull back. Keep still, dead still. He's checking this way, like he's wary of where the kid's been. He knows she came round here.

Don't think he's seen me. But I got him clear. Same greasepot as before. I'm guessing it was him and the trolls in that van. And I'll tell you something else, Bigeyes. They were looking for me. They still are.

No sign of Bex. Maybe they killed her. But they still got the kid. Look at her, Bigeyes. She's like a little flower. Beauty surrounded by shit. If they hurt her, I'll kill 'em all. If it's the last thing I do.

Riff's still looking this way. I'm starting to wonder if he's fixed me. But then Sash turns and calls out.

"Riff, come on!"

And he follows, like a good boy. Always was a flump. I watch 'em go. And I keep my eyes on Jaz long as I can. But then they're gone. Back to where I was, slump on the ground again.

And here's the tears back. She's done for me, that kid. If I was scared of the grinks, scared of the troll gang, I'm petrified of Jaz. Don't ask me why. She's not my kid. She's not even Bex's kid.

She's dead Trixi's kid. And some claphead father who's legged it. She's got no one. Just the trolls and Riff and God knows who else. I can't help her. She can't help me.

But I can't stop thinking about her.

It's no good. Got to wipe this out of my head. Got to think about me, about getting away. I made it this far. I'm close to the way out. There's a motorway service station just over two miles away. All I got to do is get there, find a lorry in the park, break into the back.

And head north. Or south. Or wherever. I can do it, Bigeyes. I can get away from here. I just got to keep low, keep out of sight, and get to the motorway service station.

So why'm I still thinking about Jaz?

Why'm I doing that, Bigeyes?

I don't want to think about Jaz, or Bex, or sweet Becky, or you, or anyone. I just want to think about me, all right? Trouble is, I can't even do that. Not properly. I keep seeing these other faces too. All of 'em. More than I can count. They won't blast out of my head.

More effing tears. Wipe my eyes, back of my sleeve. Wound's hurting again, thank Christ. I want it to. I want something else to think about. Reach up and touch the plaster. It's wet through but still on, just. But I got tiredness slamming me senseless now.

Think of the plan. Got to think of the plan. Forget Jaz. Forget all the others. Think of the plan. First things first. Get to the hideout. Eat, rest, wait till dark. Then wig it to the motorway.

Pick up the knife, close it, slip it away. Pockets bulging now. Hood up, slink to the side of the church, check round. No sign of anybody. Back to the overflow graveyard and into the trees. Cut through toward the road. Sound of a motor.

Crouch low, watch through the foliage.

Van heading back toward the city. Same grumbly engine as the one I heard before. And I was right. It's the gang. I can see Tammy sitting in the front. And Riff driving. Watch 'em go.

I'm thinking of Jaz again. She's sitting in that van, out of sight. And I can't speak to her, Bigeyes. I can't make things right. Come on. We got to get out of here. There's nothing left in this city but pain.

Cut left, down to the fence, check round. All clear. Over the fence, into the field. We got to get over to that little lane but we're keeping off the road, okay? We'll trig through the field and this part's best. Grass is longest here. But we got to play it cute. It's still easy to see us if someone's looking down from the high ground behind us.

On over the field. Pain's getting worse in my head. I feel so weak now, so full of stuff I can't handle. It's bombing me out. It's not just Jaz. It's all the grime she's making me think of. Don't know why. She doesn't mean to. She's just a kid. She didn't say a word. Just looked at me with those munchy eyes. But she's opened me up.

And I'm scared of what's inside.

Keep moving, keep bloody moving. Might help me stop thinking. Halfway across the field and there's the lane. See that wall? The lane's on the other side. Only we can't use it yet. Not in daylight. We got to wait till dark. But I know a place to hide.

Up to the wall, check round. No sign of anybody watching. Now we got to be extra cute. We got to stay out of sight. Nobody must see us, not a soul. We stay this side of the wall, and we follow the lane along to the left.

Just for a bit. The hideout's not far from here and we can rest there till dark. But we got to stay down and keep below the wall. It's a quiet lane but we're taking no chances. Not now that we're this close.

On, close to the wall. Keep down, Bigeyes. Keep right down. Field's dangerous too. The grass gets thinner farther along. But I'm hoping we're okay. Field widens as we go on and we should be too hard to see from the other end. Only danger that way is if some farmer comes sniffing about.

But it looks okay.

And now the field's opening out. Look ahead, couple of miles. See the rise? Well, the motorway's below that. This lane goes under it and the service station's a spit down from there. But that's for later. Now look just ahead. Bushes and scrub and then the wall bends round to the right, see? It's following the twist of the lane. Okay, walk on, close to the wall—and now look.

Little humpback bridge.

And a ditch underneath.

That's the hideout. Under the lane. I slept there once. And we can use it again now. Follow the wall round, stop at the bridge, check round. All's quiet, all's still. Except . . .

Listen, Bigeyes.

Birdsong.

I told you there wasn't any in the city. But I can hear some now. You got it? That's a blackbird. No messing. A beautiful blackie. And he sounds plum. Like everything's okay, everything's happy, everything's like it should be.

So why'm I crying again, Bigeyes? Eh? Tell me that.

Maybe it's cos I know deep down that it's not going to work. I'm never going to break free. Not really. Cos even if I break free from the city, from all the places I've ever been to, I'm never going to break free from being me.

I'm never going to be like Blackie.

But I still got to go. That's the crack of it, Bigeyes.

I still got to go.

Down into the ditch, under the bridge, sit on the rock. Pull out the apples and oranges and the pie. Wipe my eyes. And now that's it, Bigeyes. Nothing more to do. We sit here. We eat, we rest, we wait.

And when night comes, we're gone.

20

DARKNESS HAS COME—and with it a light.

And a new clutch of fears.

Top of the humpback bridge. Check down the lane, Big-eyes. Not toward the motorway. The other way, the way we came. Trace back down the lane to where it meets the road from the city, then follow that left for half a mile.

See the light?

All on its own?

Just gone out. You probably missed it. Well, I didn't. And I'll tell you what it's from. A motorbike. Tell you something else too. Whoever's on it knows where we are.

Which means other nebs do too.

You're thinking it's just a light. Could be anyone. Nothing to do with us. Well, you're wrong. It's grinks. And there'll be lots of 'em. They won't take any chances this time. And they won't just be back there. They'll be all round. They'll be making a big, big circle. And closing in.

Can't see 'em yet. Too dark and no stars or moon tonight. That'll make it hard for us. Hard for them too but they got it easier than we have. Cos there's so many of them. They'll stretch the circle all the way out to the motorway, all the way round the fields, every direction, and then move in slow.

We won't see 'em till the last minute.

Maybe it was Riff tipped 'em. He was their screamer last time. He's probably done it again. Spotted me peeping round the edge of the church after Jaz. Made like he didn't, drove off, rang 'em up. Left me to 'em. And now they're taking their time. But they'll all be in place and they'll be moving already, snuffing the air out of the circle.

And all the hope out of my life.

Come on, Bigeyes. We can't stay here.

Walk, down the lane. Yeah, I know. You're thinking why not the field where it's more hidden? Cos it won't work now. Trust me. The field's no place for us. It's just one big open space.

Lane's not much better.

But there's a little hamlet just ahead. Cluster of houses and a shop, closed down. And something else. Something I want. Won't save my life. But I've given up on that now anyway. Keep walking, keep watching. We can't get away. I know it. But I want to see 'em coming. I want to see their faces.

Still no sign yet. Just the dark lane stretching away. Blackie's out there too somewhere. I like the thought of that. Wonder what he's doing. Sitting quiet in some leafy snug, I hope. Knowing he's going to sing again tomorrow.

There's that light again, Bigeyes.

Behind you, see it? The motorbike light. It's moved but it's still keeping well back. I didn't even hear the engine. Maybe I'm losing my touch. Gone off again. Only now I can see figures moving in the darkness.

They're here sooner than I thought.

Check round. Just like I said. A big, big circle. Out in the fields, all around. And there'll be loads I can't see. They maybe haven't spotted me yet. But they will soon. They can't miss. I'm dead, Bigeyes. There's no way out of this.

But I can still do one thing.

If I'm quick.

Here's the hamlet. Houses well back from the lane, lights off. Like the nebs inside know there's going to be trouble. Only they don't. How could they? They're probably just sleeping. It's old nebs who live out here. I've seen 'em. Well, I'm glad they're tucked up cozy. I hope they stay that way.

There's too many people died cos of me.

On to the little shop, boarded up. And here's what I came for.

The phone booth.

Better be working. Open the door, check the dial tone. It's cute. Now I'm glad I had some coins in my safe. Pull 'em out. Not many but enough. Push in some coins, dial. Woman answers, starts the spiel. I cut in quick.

"Give me the number for The Crown on South Street."

"Which town or city?"

I tell her. She goes quiet. I'm watching the darkness through the glass of the phone booth. She comes back.

"Would you like me to connect you?"

"Just do it quick."

"There's no need to be—"

"Just put me through, can you?"

She gives a snort but puts me through. Sound of a phone ringing, then another woman's voice.

"The Crown?"

I take a breath. Got to sound polite or she'll crash me out.

"Can I speak to Jacob, please?"

I'm praying she'll just get him. She doesn't answer. Sound of voices in the background, pubby voices. Then a gobbo, old, gravelly, Irish.

"This is Jacob."

"I need to speak to Mary."

Another silence. I try again.

"Please. I need to speak to Mary."

"I don't know anyone called Mary."

"Mary, Lily, whatever she calls herself. Tell her it's a friend of Buffy's."

Yet another silence. Far down the lane I can see the motor-bike light again. It's closer but it's just stuck there. Goes out again. I see shadows moving into the hamlet.

Hear a voice on the line.

"Blade?"

It's Mary. And now I can't speak.

"Is that you?" she says.

"Yeah."

I'm watching the shadows. They've stopped some way back. Pretty sure they've seen me now. They're just waiting. Gathering all the others probably, just to make sure I can't get away. Twist round, check the other way.

More shadows coming from the other end. They've stopped too. And there's more coming over the fields. Mary speaks again, quietly, deliberately.

"There have been two murders in the last twenty-four hours."

"I didn't do 'em. But . . ."

"But what?"

I don't answer. I can't.

"But what?" she says again.

I still can't answer. She speaks again.

"But you know something about them? Is that what you're saying?"

Silence.

"Or maybe something else?" she says. "Maybe . . . you've done something like that yourself?"

I'm frozen now. But it's too late. I can't go back. She's walked right into my head without me saying anything.

"You've killed someone," she says. "Haven't you?"

"I got to go."

"Maybe more than one person."

"I got to go."

"Then why haven't you hung up already?"

I don't know, Bigeyes. Why haven't I?

Another silence. She speaks again.

"Why have you phoned me?"

"You said I could. You said you couldn't promise to help me. But you promised to listen."

"I'm listening."

Only now I can't talk, Bigeyes. I can't say anything. I don't know what I wanted to say anyway. Maybe I just wanted to tell her . . . I don't know . . . that I'm not totally, totally evil.

But maybe I am. Maybe that's why I can't speak.

"Blade," she says, "you've got to give yourself up. Are you listening? You've got to face up to the law. You've got to face up to yourself."

"I've done too much." I'm watching the shadows move closer. "Too many bad things."

"Then you need to stop running. Running won't make any of those things right. You've phoned me because you feel bad. Because you've got a conscience. That's a good thing. That's a hopeful thing. So now do the next hopeful thing. Go to the police and tell them all the things you've done, and take responsibility."

More shadows. Too many to bother counting. They're all around me. A wall of grinks. Closing in.

Mary speaks again.

"There were two things you were right about."

I don't answer. I'm watching the shadows edging forward.

"The bungalow wasn't mine," she goes on. "It belongs to a family I saw going away on holiday. I'd just arrived and I was desperate for somewhere to stay. Somewhere secret where I couldn't be traced. I saw them catching a bus to the airport and made a note of their address from one of the luggage labels. I felt bad about using their bungalow. But I had to. Because of the second thing you were right about."

"You're on the run."

"Yes, but not from the police. From other people. I came to the city to find someone. I won't say any more. Except that I'm not a criminal. And that's why I'm not being hypocritical when I urge you to give yourself up to the police."

"It's too late for that."

"It's not. Phone them. Do it now."

"The only person I ever want to phone is you."

I don't know why I said that. Sounds stupid. The shadows move even closer. Mary speaks again.

"You won't be able to phone me much longer."

"Why not? You going away?"

"In a manner of speaking."

"What does that mean?"

She's quiet for a moment. Then she comes back. Her voice sounds so soft, so Irish, so beautiful.

"Put it this way—the doctor gave me three weeks. And that was four weeks ago."

Beeps in the phone. I crash another coin in.

"Blade," she says. "Go to the police. Please. Do the right thing. Do it for me. Do it for yourself."

The phone goes dead. She's hung up. I push open the door, step out onto the lane. It's dark with figures now. No flashlights, no faces. Just scum, creeping close.

And then I hear it.

The roar of the engine. A light flares over me. I stare down the lane, past the moving figures, and there's the motorbike, and it's a big'un, a great, bellowing beast of a machine. I can see the rider hunched over, helmet shining in the night.

The bike thunders forward. It's close to the wall of grinks now. They're turning, bracing themselves, but it scatters 'em easy as it bursts through. And now it's racing straight for me. I jump back, press myself against the phone booth. The shadows are moving forward again, but I'm watching the bike.

It squeals to a halt beside me.

"Get on!" says the rider.

A gobbo's voice, gruff. Can't see his face but I don't care. I'm on the bike, I'm clutching the rack, and he's revving up already. Now the grinks come running. I cling on, watching 'em loom close. They won't scatter this time. I duck, ready for the blows.

But they never come. With a growl of the engine we burst through and out the other side. And here's the lane stretching away, cut through by the beam of the light, and we're racing on, into the night, into a darkness I'm scared to see.

21

THE NIGHT, THE MOTORBIKE, the twisting lane. The beam from the headlights stabbing the dark. It might as well be stabbing me. Cos I'm dead all over again. I know it. I'm hurtling through blackness, perched on the back seat.

I don't even know the rider. I heard his voice, caught his eyes under the helmet. That's all. But I know enough. I jumped on like he told me to. Right thing to do cos it got us past the grinks. But it's only putting death off for a bit.

Cos this guy's a grink too.

Trust me. I got too many enemies. And no friends. So work it out for yourself. This gobbo's trouble. Big trouble too, dangerous. You don't risk your neck like he did for nothing. He gritted it big-time to get me away. So what does he want?

Whatever it is, Bigeyes, it'll be messy.

I'm guessing a contract job. I told you before there's different types of grinks. There's the ones who want me for stuff I know. Once they've tortured that out of me, they'll stiff me. And there's the ones who want me for stuff I've done. I'm hoping they'll just stiff me quick and sweet.

But I don't suppose I'll be that lucky.

I'm guessing this gobbo's one of the second kind. Sent by some spike from the past who's got a grudge against me.

There's enough of 'em. I turned over too many slugs to have a quiet life. Maybe I turned over one of his crew. So he sent this gobbo to get me.

And now it's payback.

Going to be bad, Bigeyes, whatever happens. And I'm weak as piss now. Wound in my head's slamming me, body's blasted after all the chasing, and my mind's stuffed after seeing Jaz and talking to Mary. What's left to fight another grink?

Not much. Maybe not anything.

But I still got some kind of a chance. That's why I jumped on the bike. This way there's just two of us. For the moment anyway. Won't be for long but right now it's him against me. Better odds than before. So I'm clinging on and hoping. He's got to stop sometime.

And that's when I'll know what to do.

Fight or run.

Or both.

We're still moving fast. This is some machine, I'm telling you, and the gobbo's some rider. I'll give him that. I'm checking him best I can. Big guy, solid. More beef than your average dronk.

Glance behind me. Thought so. Headlights coming after us. Only they're not motorbikes. They're cars. And there'll be more coming the other way in a minute. The grinks back there'll have mobiled their mates. Second wave, case I got through the first.

So this motorbike gobbo's in trouble too, whatever he wants from me. And he'll have to do something soon cos the motorway's just ahead, and there'll be a reception committee. Only wait a second . . .

He's switched off the lights and we're slowing down. We're still moving but there's darkness all around now. I don't like this. Can't see a thing hardly. Glance back.

Headlights getting bigger. They're racing after us but they're still some way off. Lights ahead of us too now, coming from the direction of the motorway. But we're still running through darkness.

Only now we're turning off the lane. We've slipped through an open gate—I can just make it out—and we're bumping down a track with a field to the left and a fence to the right. Peer at the rider.

He hasn't looked round once, hasn't checked to see what I'm doing or who's following. He's bent forward like he's been from the start, his helmet gleaming. But that's all the light that's coming from us now.

The bike's as dark as the night.

We're still bumping along the track, and now there's another gate in front, open too, and we're through that, and we're on another track, heading toward some trees. Maybe that's it, Bigeyes. Maybe that's where his mates'll be waiting.

Where it all ends.

A club, knife, bullet. Cute little grave. No one'll find me if they do it right. Look behind me again. Lights flashing down the lane, both directions. None of 'em coming our way.

But they will. They'll know we haven't got as far as the motorway. They'll regroup and come looking. They'll search every gate and every field. Yeah, Bigeyes, they want me that bad. But I got other problems now.

Check round. Still too risky to jump off the bike. We're going slower but not so slow I won't hurt myself if I try and bunk it. Got to wait a bit longer. Track's come to an end but he's driving on. We're in among the trees, bouncing along, lights still off.

Then suddenly he pulls up.

We're in a little clearing. Nobody else around, nobody I can see anyway. I scramble off the bike, scuttle back a few steps. Guy glances round, climbs off, clicks the bike onto its stand. Stares at me through the slit in his helmet. Then he moves.

I edge back farther, but not too far. Got to watch this gobbo every second. If he's working on his own, that's better for me but it's still bad. He's big and strong and I won't get away by running. Even if I wasn't weak, I couldn't outpace him.

Got to wait, watch, see what he wants.

He's stopped by the back of the bike but he's still looking this way. I'm watching him cute. There's something about this guy. I've only just noticed. Something in his manner. I've seen him before somewhere.

But I can't work out where.

We're both still now, both staring hard. Behind him, where the lane cuts toward the motorway, I catch the flash of headlights. I can't see the cars. They're hidden below the rise of the land. But I can see the beams. And this gobbo must know they're there too. But he's not looking at them. He's keeping his eyes on me.

I call over.

"You're either brave or stupid."

He doesn't answer, just goes on staring at me. I peer through the darkness at the slit in his helmet. Can't make out his eyes from here but I got a sense of 'em. Maybe if I could see 'em better, I could work out where I've met him. But that means trigging closer and I'm not that big a dimp.

I nod toward the lane.

"They're going to want you now. Not just me."

Again he doesn't answer. Just reaches out, opens the panier at the back of the bike and pulls out another helmet. Then, without warning, he flings it over. I don't try and catch it. Just let it land close to my feet, then bend down and pick it up. He closes the panier, steps in front of the bike, faces me across the clearing.

"What do you want?" I say.

He nods to the helmet in my hands.

"Put it on. You need to look legal."

And then I get it. The voice. It wasn't enough before, when he told me to get on the bike. It was gruff and hurried and there wasn't time to think. But now it's different. Just those few words, but I can hear the drawl. And I know who it is.

He doesn't need to do any more. But he does anyway. He pulls off his helmet and lets me see his face.

It's Dig.

22

DEAD TRIXI'S BROTHER. Twenty years old and tough as two men. The guy who sliced my head with his knife. And there it is again. He's pulled it out. The blade looks even bigger than it did when he slashed me. Maybe it's still got my blood on it.

I reach in my pocket, feel for Scumbo's knife.

It's there, ready.

Only I can't pull it out. It's no good, Bigeyes. I got those feelings back, like I had with Paddy and that other grink. Only it's worse now. I can't even pull the knife out. If Dig throws his, he's got a free plug.

And he does. He throws it.

I watch it skin the dark as it streaks toward me. Don't know why I haven't moved. Maybe I want it to slam me. But it doesn't. It dips at the last moment and stabs into the grass between my feet.

I look down at it, then up at Dig.

He didn't miss. He aimed it there. He could have slotted me easy. I'm near enough. But he didn't. Why not? I already know, Bigeyes. It's cos he's confident I can't hurt him back. Even with his own knife.

I lean down, pick it up, study it. One mean blade. No wonder I got hurt when he slit me. Heavy too, much heavier than Trixi's flick knife, or the one in my pocket. Once upon a time I'd have liked it. Squeeze my hand round it, look at Dig, size him up. Move my arm back.

He stiffens.

I hold still. I want to see him scared. He owes me that. But he doesn't flinch. Just watches me for a moment, checks me over, then settles his body, lounges, waits. He's got bottle. I'll give him that. I hate the guy but he's crack-hard.

I take a step toward him. He stiffens again. Now he's not sure. Now I've got him. But still he won't move. I want him to step back, step aside, something. But he doesn't. Just waits like before, watching me in the darkness. Then he speaks, same low drawl.

"You ain't going to do it."

I take another step forward. Still he doesn't move. I wait, watching him. I'm so close now I could hit him blind. He gives me the drawl again.

"You ain't going to do it. And you know it."

I got pictures flooding my head again, and they're all faces. Paddy's face, and the scumbo in the hospital, and those two grinks I saw on the old dunny's staircase. All mocking me the same way. Cos I can't do it anymore.

Can't kill.

And now Dig's face. How come he knows? Is it the grinks? Did they tell him? Or is it just me, standing here, showing it in my face? We're close enough now. He can see my eyes dead clear. Just as I can see his. Dead clear.

They're watching me cute, but they're quiet eyes, relaxed eyes. Not scared at all. I drop the helmet to the ground, whip the knife right back over my shoulder. Still he doesn't flinch. Still the eyes go on watching me. Then he shakes his head.

"Ain't going to happen. Cos you ain't standing much longer."

He's right, Bigeyes. I'm swaying on my feet and the world's spinning again. I got pain blacking me over, and fear, and exhaustion. And there's more pictures splitting my head— sweet Becky, her dead face peering up, and all the others, the faces I can't bear to see. The faces that never go away.

And Dig's among them, watching.

I feel myself drop the knife. The faces start whirling, the blackness deepens. I don't remember falling, just waking up, I don't know how much later. I'm staring into Dig's face. He's holding me and I hate it.

"Let go," I mutter.

He doesn't. I scream at him.

"Let go! Let go!"

I got new pictures flashing, pictures from the past, pictures that freak my heart.

"Let go! Let go! Let go!"

He still goes on holding me. I spit into his face. He twists his head away, carries me over to the motorbike, dumps me on the passenger seat, wipes the gob off with his sleeve. I glare at him but I'm losing it again. I'm upright, sort of, but my head's still spinning and I can feel the blacko creeping back.

Dig speaks.

"Blade."

His voice has turned into mist.

"You got to hold on," he says. "Got to stay conscious, you understand? Cos we got to start riding again. And if you lose it, you'll fall off."

I can't see him at all now. I feel something over my head. The helmet, he's putting it on me. Now my hands. He's grabbed hold of 'em.

"Don't touch me," I say.

He takes no notice, moves my hands behind me, closes the fingers round something cold.

"It's the bike rack," he says. "Hold on to it."

I grip the rack.

"Now your feet," he says.

"Don't touch 'em. I know where they go."

Again he takes no notice. Just plants my feet, climbs on in front of me, speaks again.

"Don't let go, boy. Or you're dead."

He pauses, like he's waiting for me to say something. But I can't speak, Bigeyes. I can't even think. I'm losing everything. I got a little bit left in me. Maybe enough to hang on, maybe not. I don't really care now.

I just want him to ride.

Somewhere, anywhere.

Doesn't matter where it is now. Or what he wants from me.

"Ride," I mutter.

He starts the engine. It brays like a monster. I can't believe the grinks on the lane won't have heard it. But he's not heading their way. Even in this state, I can tell that. He's kicked off the stand and we're bumping on through the trees, lights still off.

I don't know where he's going, Bigeyes.

And you know what? I don't give two bells.

My eyes are closing and it's like I'm gone. I'm not Blade. I'm not a fourteen-year-old kid clinging to the back of a motorbike. I'm not anyone. I'm just a thought moving through darkness.

I like that.

A thought moving through darkness.

The world's gone, life's gone. Blade's gone.

I just hope he never comes back.

23

BUT HE DOES. Course he does, damn the bastard. He's like a curse. Even as I flake, I feel him hovering. Like you, Bigeyes—hovering. And there's others too. And I'm not talking about Dig.

Something's happened. There's more nebs round me. Bike's gone. Don't know where. I remember the trees but that's it. Don't remember the journey after that or getting off. Just know I'm somewhere else, it's dark in my head, and I can't move.

And I'm scared.

I can hear voices but no words. And something else, kind of a drone. Keep thinking I should know what it is. But my head's bombed and my thoughts are sprung. They got no shape, no sense.

Like me.

Then a word. Clear as sky. And someone's speaking it.

"Jaz."

And now a picture. The little girl's face. She's looking at me with those fairy eyes. Not smiling or crying, not telling me it's all right. Just watching. I don't know if she's real or in my head. Voice comes again.

"Jaz."

It's not Jaz talking. It's some girl, older. I'm getting more pictures now. I'm starting to remember. I'm guessing where

I am and who I'm with. But I still can't see 'em. All I got is Jaz. But that's okay. Cos she's all I want.

I try and speak.

"Jaz, I'm sorry, baby."

She doesn't answer. Don't know if she heard. The other voice comes back.

"Jaz, come on."

Jaz disappears and all I got is darkness again, and the blur of voices, and the drone in the background. I know what it is now. I know what's happening. I'm in a van. And Blade's still here, locked inside me. He'll never go away, Bigeyes, no matter how much I want him to.

Think I'm losing it again, going blacko like before. I can feel it swimming over me. And I want it now. I want to forget again. For a while I wasn't me and it was plum. The black tide washes in, sweeps me away, rolls me up.

But not for long.

I'm soon back, dumped where I was, like a piece of driftwood. And that's how it feels now. I'm floating. I go with the current. I got no control over anything. And I know the nebs I'm with, even if I can't see 'em. Engine's getting louder, and now there's other sounds.

Sirens.

Must be porkers everywhere. All these murders in the city. Maybe the sirens'll help a bit, keep the grinks back. Getting louder, one of 'em. Louder, louder, louder. Dead close now, blaring over us, and light from the headlights flooding the van.

Sound of voices nearby. I recognize 'em good this time.

The trolls talking.

"They're getting too close."

"Might not be after us."

"They is."

"Might be turning off."

"They ain't. They're checking us out."

Another voice, a guy in the front.

"They're turning off."

And the light fades away, taking the siren with it.

Something's touching my head, dabbing at me, something soft. Doesn't feel like a hand but I can't make it out.

"Stay still."

Tammy's voice. No missing that. She's taken over as leader, now that Trixi's dead. Don't ask me how I know. Sash won't like it. Nor will Xen and Kat. But they won't challenge her. She was always the strongest after Trixi.

Not that any of that's going to help me. Trolls are trolls and this crew's always hated me. If they're patching me up, it's only so I'm fit for something worse.

"Stay still," says Tammy.

I didn't know I was moving.

"Open your eyes," she says.

Didn't know they were closed either. I open 'em. Still blackness all around me. No faces, just shapes. Then one, clear. Not Tammy or any of the other trolls. It's Jaz again. And she's real. She's right next to me.

"Jaz," I whisper.

I can feel my mind splitting again and the blacko coming back. Got to keep it away. Got to keep my eyes on Jaz. She reaches out, pats at my forehead, and then I know what's been dabbing me. She's holding an old sweater. Tammy's voice again.

"Your wound's bleeding."

And now her troll face, glaring down. I always hated it. Spitty eyes, no friends of mine. She looks me over, growls.

"Keep still."

Glances at Jaz.

"Give me the thing."

Jaz hands her the sweater. Tammy nods toward the front of the van.

"Go sit with Riff."

Jaz disappears. I close my eyes, feel the sweater on my brow again.

"You should be dead," says Tammy.

"Why aren't I?"

"Good question."

Yeah, Bigeyes, good question. She's right. I should be dead. Breaking free should have cost me my life. But maybe it has. Maybe the next blacko'll be it. The one I don't come back from.

I thought I was dead before. In the ambulance, in the hospital, in Scumbo's black arms. And then later—on the rooftops, in the streets, running, running. But how long can you run when you're hurt that bad?

Cos I was, and I still am. I know that.

"Bleeding's gross," says Tammy.

I don't answer. She's not talking to me anyway.

"Tam?" says Sash.

"What?"

"Can't you stop it?"

"I'm trying, aren't I?"

"I was just asking."

"You wasn't. You was telling me I'm doing a shit job."

"Hey!" calls Riff from the front of the van. "Shut it, you two!"

"You shut it," says Tammy.

"You babes are always rowing."

"So what?"

"So don't," says Riff. "You know Dig hates it."

"Well, he ain't here, is he?" says Tammy. "So piss off!"

Riff says no more. Sash speaks, low voice.

"Bleeding's getting worse."

No answer from Tammy, just the feel of the sweater again, and the blood flowing down my face. The sirens seem far away now. I can still hear 'em but they're like voices from another world. Here comes the blacko again.

At last.

Come on, mate. Fold me up. I've had enough of this. And I don't mean the trolls slugging, or the pain, or the stuff they got waiting for me. I mean everything. Every thing. Let the blood flow all it wants.

Cos you know what, Bigeyes? I owe it. Too right I do. I owe more blood than I got in my body. Maybe if it all drains away, I'll have given something back. Not enough for what I owe. Not by a long way. But maybe enough to get a bit of peace.

And there's something else too.

I'll be dead.

And you don't get more peaceful than that.

24

LIGHT. CONSCIOUSNESS. A new movement. A new kind of fear.

I'm on water.

I can tell. I'm alive and I'm on water. Wound's stopped bleeding but something else is running down my cheek. It's sweat. Got my eyes wide open but all I can see is a blur. Light's clear but nothing else is. Just the feeling of water.

And my fear of it.

"Drowning."

I'm murmuring. I can hear my own voice. Doesn't sound like me. Sounds like some dungpot with his head banged in. But it is me. I know it. More sweat. I can feel the beads on my neck now.

Close my eyes, open 'em again.

Light's still there, but now I can see stuff. Inside of a cabin: small, smoky, little round portholes. I'm lying on a bunk with a blanket over me. I don't remember coming here. Nobody else with me. Nobody I can see anyway.

But I'm not alone.

There's sounds coming from behind my head. Twist round. Painful to move but I manage it. Closed door that way, another cabin probably. And the sounds are coming from there. No mistaking what's going on.

Some couple making out.

Twist my head back. Boat rocks. Feel my body tense.

Another rock of the boat. I start to tremble. I can feel the water close, like it's breathing up through the boat—into my face, into my heart.

"No!" I scream.

Sounds break off in the other cabin. Door opens, figure stumbles out. Riff, doing up his trousers. Another figure, one of the trolls. Can't remember her name. I'm still drowning in my head. She straightens her kit, puts a hand on my cheek.

"Lay off!" I snarl.

She takes her hand away. I glare at her. Name comes back. Kat, that's it. She's watching me close. Gritty eyes but better than Tammy's. Snap of warmth in 'em. Not much but a bit. And she can do better than Riff for a bed-bum.

Check him out, Bigeyes. Proper slimeball. I'm not forgetting he shunted me with Paddy and those other grinks. Question is—what's his jig now? I got to think, got to hold back this fear. I'm out of strength. Got no spit left in my body.

But I'm still alive. Don't ask me why. And there's another thing.

Where's the rest of the gang?

Riff answers my question like I spoke it out loud.

"There's nobody else here. Just me and Kat."

I don't answer. I'm still trying to think.

"You screamed," says Kat. "What's up?"

Still don't answer, still trying to think. Sound of an engine roaring past. Riff checks through the porthole, looks back.

"Nothing," he says to Kat.

Then the swell hits us. Boat starts to rock. I can't help it. I'm screaming again.

"No! No!"

"Easy," says Kat.

She reaches out.

"Don't touch me!"

"Okay, okay." She takes her hand away, stands back.

Both watching me now, narrowed eyes, like they don't know what to do. Sweat's pouring down me like a flood. Boat settles and I calm down a bit.

"Blade," says Riff.

"Shove it."

"Blade, listen."

I scowl at him. He takes no notice, leans forward. I see his eyes clear. Dark little dots, flicking about. He smiles. But it's not a proper smile. Just a mouth moving. Like the eyes. Fixed on nothing, worth nothing.

"You're ill, Blade."

"Shove it."

"You're ill. You're badly hurt. I know why you're scared. You think we're going to kill you. Well, we ain't. We know about Trixi. We know who killed her. We know it wasn't you."

I turn my head away. I can't bear to look at these two. I just want 'em to go. I want to think, make sense of all this, deal with the water, deal with what's in my head. I hear Kat speak, but not to me. She's whispering to Slimey.

"He's scared stiff."

Riff grunts.

"Blade?" says Kat. "We ain't going to hurt you."

I'm trembling again. Can't stop. If I could just get off this water. But I'm stuck here, too weak to move, too weak to think almost. It's not just the wound Dig fizzed in my head. It's what it cost me breaking free.

Cos it was everything, Bigeyes. Everything I had. And all

for this, all for nothing. There's just one thing left worth caring about now. I turn my head back to 'em.

"Where's Jaz?"

Kat and Riff look at each other.

"Where's Jaz?" I say.

Kat answers.

"Bex is looking after her."

I close my eyes. It's good for a moment cos I can see the little girl's face in the darkness. Not smiling but safe. Safe in my head anyway. Then I feel something on my cheek. It's not Kat's hand. It's something cold.

Familiar.

"Take it away," I say.

I don't open my eyes. I just wait. It stays there for a moment, then goes away. I open my eyes and see Riff closing the blade of the flick knife. The one I had in my coat pocket. Along with the other stuff.

"I was trying to show you," he says.

"Show me what?"

"That we're not going to hurt you. I was trying to give you back your knife."

"I had my eyes closed. How would I know you weren't trying to slit me?"

"But I didn't, did I? Like you say, you had your eyes closed. You were an easy target. If I'd wanted to cut your throat, we wouldn't be talking now."

His eyes dance over me.

"Here," he says. He holds out the knife, closed now. "I just wanted to make you see what I'm doing. So I can give this back to you."

I don't take it. He rests it on the bunk, straightens up.

"So you've been through my pockets?" I say.

He doesn't answer, just glances at Kat. I try again.

"What you done with the other stuff?"

"Like what?"

"Like the other stuff."

"You mean the twelve and a half grand?"

"Yeah. I mean the twelve and a half grand."

He shrugs.

"Call it rent."

"You bastard."

"For safe custody."

"You bastard."

The eyes stop moving for a second, then flicker on.

"You might think it money well spent," he says, "when you consider how much danger we're keeping you from." He leans closer. "There's police everywhere looking for you. And God knows how many other people. Nasty people too. We don't know who they are. Maybe you're going to tell us."

"Maybe I'm not."

"Whoever they are, they're not very friendly. But you don't need me to tell you that, do you?"

The boat rocks again. I clutch the side of the bunk and my hand touches the knife. I close it inside my grip, squeeze it tight. Boat goes on rocking, then slowly settles again. I hold up the knife, flick it open.

Kat stiffens. Riff just smiles.

"There's no point hurting us, Blade. Cos we're all that's keeping you safe now. You need us on your side." He shakes his head. "Look at you. You're wounded. You're knackered. And you're running scared."

I stare at the blade for a moment, then twist my hand and

slam the point down into the bunk. The knife quivers for a few seconds, then falls still. I glower up at Riff.

"You'll be running scared soon. And the rest of your crew."

"And why's that?" he says.

I pause, fix 'em both.

"Cos the shit that's coming after me's coming after you now."

25

THEY FEED ME: sandwiches from a plastic bag, couple of apples, unripe banana. Give me a bottle of mineral water. I eat, drink a bit, fall asleep. When I wake, it's dark again, and I'm alone.

Except for you, Bigeyes. And the stinky water. I got a woolly hat on my head and the bandage is still on. Or maybe it's another bandage. Don't know. It's wet anyway.

I'm on my feet—managed that after a struggle—but I got nothing in my legs. Nothing much anyway. Just enough to stand, check out the boat, slop over to the porthole, stare out.

Familiar sight. Moorings, boats swinging with the tide, lights from the shore quarter of a mile away. I know this place well enough. Back end of the city, where the river gobs into the sea. But I've never seen it from the water before.

Don't have to tell you why.

Least I've stopped trembling. That's one good thing. But I still choke up every time the boat heaves. And it does that a lot. This is one slaggy tub. Supposed to be a motor cruiser but it's more of a floating wreck. Two dronky cabins and a wheelhouse. Smell of diesel and rotting timber. Bits of rope and chain. Stuff all else.

And no dinghy to get me ashore.

I don't remember Riff and Kat going. Must have been sleeping when they split. But I'm glad they've gone. I might be stuck here on my own but it's about as safe as anywhere else right now, long as I stay inside the cabin.

And I'm cute about that. You better believe it. Cos I'm telling you, Bigeyes, there's no way I'm going out on deck, not with the water that close. I can just about handle it from in here. So I'll slap it in the cabin for now. I got to stay out of sight anyway.

Just wish I could stay out of mind too. Cos that's the crack of it, Bigeyes. I'm in too many people's heads now. Porkers, grinks, you name it, all sniffing my tracks. I got to watch every shadow.

Something's moving on the water.

Can't see it yet but I can hear an engine. Not loud, just an outboard motor probably, some way off. Coming from the right. Check out the portholes. Nothing. Just the water and the lights from the shore.

Boat's getting closer. Still quiet, just a hum, but it's slowing down. There it is. Black shape moving through the moorings. I was wrong. It's not got an outboard motor. It's a launch with a little doghouse and a chuggy engine down below.

Three figures in the cockpit.

One of 'em's the grunt.

There's no missing that gobbo. Even in the dark I can see his fat face. Check round, reach for the bunk. Knife's still stuck in it. Pull it out, squeeze the handle, turn back to the porthole.

Launch has slowed down further but it's still moving. Not coming this way but weaving about, checking the moored boats inshore. I'm watching cute. They're over by the cruiser with the tatty awning.

Peering through the portholes.

One of 'em's climbing on board, checking under the cover. Now he's back in the launch. Rev of the engine and they're off again, but only to the next boat. And it's the same again.

Shit, Bigeyes. If they check this dingo, I'm clemmed.

And they will. They're grubbing out all the bigger boats. They'll do this one too. Least I got no lights on. And the grinks don't seem to know which boat I'm on cos they're slugging all of 'em. Some screamer's tipped 'em off, I reckon, but not with any details or they wouldn't be checking rough-cut.

Even so, I got to hide.

Only where? Cabins won't do, nor will the wheelhouse. Loo's too obvious. So there's one choice left and it's a bum gripe. I'm not going there till I know I got to. Peer out the porthole.

Careful.

Got to keep 'em in view but stay out of sight. Yeah, they're checking everything. Not just the big boats now. They're even grubbing out the littl'uns. Just a poke in but enough to make sure.

They're coming this way.

Quick!

Knife down, coat on, knife back in my hand, check round. Just the food and mineral water to show 'em I was here. Shove the banana skin and apple core into the plastic bag. Stuff it in one pocket, bottle in the other.

Engine's getting louder.

Creep to the front of the cabin, up into the wheelhouse, keeping low. Pause, listen. They're almost alongside now. Down into the engine room. Only it's not an engine room. It's a greasy cupboard you wouldn't force a rat in.

But I got to hide there.

Somehow.

Ease my body in, twist it round over the engine, close the little door after me, hold it tight. As I do so, I hear the grinks climb on board.

All three. I'm sure of it. Starboard side's gone right down. Even the grunt couldn't do that on his own. Engine's still chugging alongside but I'm guessing they've tied up and come aboard.

Three grinks.

And me.

Shit.

Footsteps on the deck. Boat's back on an even keel. The grinks are spreading about. In a moment they'll see the hatchway's open and find their way down into the cabins. Then they'll check out the wheelhouse.

And the engine room.

A voice, clear over the sound of the engine. And I know it at once. That familiar grunty sound.

"Hatchway's unlocked."

Sound of the hatchway being pulled back. Footsteps thumping down into the cabin I was in. Bang of a door as someone checks the other cabin. Another bang as he comes out again. More footsteps.

Heading for the wheelhouse.

There's three of 'em. I was right. I can tell from the footsteps. First grink's in the wheelhouse, now the second, now the third. I can see one of 'em through a gap in the door. Just a tiny bit, the outside of a boot.

In a moment the door's going to yank open.

And they'll have me.

Grunt speaks.

"I can see him."

"Blade?" says another.

"Yeah."

"Where is he?"

He's playing with me, Bigeyes. And he's playing with his mates. He's spotted the little door. They all have. You can't miss it. But he's the one who's worked out I'm behind it. He must have seen me through the gap. Squeeze my hand round the knife.

If I can just get some of my old bottle back . . .

It's a long shot and they'll still get me. But I might be able to take one of 'em first. Grunt speaks again.

"There."

He's got to be pointing down at the door.

"On the shore," he says. "See?"

No answer from his mates, just a rush of footsteps, a smash of the wheelhouse door as they blast it open, then a rev of the engine.

And they're powering off toward the shore.

26

JESUS, BIGEYES, I'M THANKING THAT GUY. The guy they think is me. I just hope nothing happens to him. But whoever he is, I owe him.

Okay, got to hold on a bit, got to wait.

Got to be sure. Engine's fading quick cos they're ripping up. That's good cos I want 'em gone, but I still got to wait. Got to play stealth. No matter how much I hate this cupboard.

Give it another minute. Got to be sure, dead sure. Another minute, another. Now it's cute. Shove open the door, fall back into the wheelhouse. I'm rolling on the floor, breathing hard, and—shit, Bigeyes. I'm crying again.

What's the matter with me?

I can't crack this, Bigeyes. The tears and stuff. I never used to cry. Not after I toughed out. Up to age seven, yeah. Tears, plenty of 'em. Then nothing. Not a drop, not even when Becky died. I wanted to but I knocked 'em back. You got to do that or you're bombed.

Are you listening to this, Bigeyes?

You knock 'em back or they knock you back. You're finished. You don't make it. Only now I can't stop 'em. Ever since the grinks came back, and Bex and Jaz and Mary came into my life, it's like they brought the tears with 'em.

So now what?

Stay alive. That's what. Cos I'll tell you something, Bigeyes.

It's not about winning. It's about staying alive. You know why? Cos you don't win against these nebs. Most of the time you don't stay alive either.

Not if you go against 'em. There's too many grinks out there. And too many spikes pulling their strings. And up above the spikes, the meanest slime of the lot. We're talking serious shit, Bigeyes. Trust me. Serious shit. And it's not just this country.

It's global.

I'm telling you, there's nebs out there with everything to lose if I stay free. Why? Cos there's stuff I know, stuff they want, stuff other people want, including the porkers. But that's not the most dangerous thing. The most dangerous thing is something I don't know.

The person at the very top.

But never mind that now. I got to crash these tears, get my head straight, check Grunty and his mates have gone. Over to the wheelhouse door. It's hanging limp, half off its hinges. Keep low, peer out.

There's the launch, moored up against the old barge. No sign of the grinks. They didn't hang about. Must have climbed ashore and run after the guy they thought was me. So I got to be careful and keep watching.

Cos when they find out it's not me, they'll come back.

And go on looking.

They might even come back here.

I hate this, Bigeyes. I feel so trapped. And I hate this water. It feels closer than ever now with the door pushed out of the way. I can see its black face right in front of me. Maybe it can see mine. Maybe I'm not the only one who's scared. Maybe the water's scared too. Scared of me even.

Don't think so though.

"Are you scared of me?" My voice sounds weird. Like a whisper and a scream at the same time. "Eh? Are you scared?"

The water doesn't answer. Just wrinkles its dark skin. I shiver.

"I'm scared of you. I don't mind admitting it. I'm cute about that."

A ripple runs over the surface, dies under the boat.

I push the door back farther, bend down closer to the deck, edge myself over the threshold. I'm on hands and knees now. Can't bring myself to stand. Not just cos the grinks might see me if they come back. If they weren't around, I'd still be on hands and knees.

And you know why.

Inch toward the gunwale, still close to the deck. Don't ask me why I'm doing this. Maybe if the water told me it was scared too, I'd be braver. But it hasn't, so I'm not. But I got to get closer somehow.

Got to stare this bastard down.

Ease myself farther. I'm flat out now, pulling myself over the deck, eyes tight shut. I didn't want 'em like that, but I can't help it. They closed by themselves and I can't force 'em back open.

Never mind.

I'll do it in a minute. When I get there. Just a bit farther. I'm moving slower, fighting the will to stop, but then suddenly I'm there. I can feel my head brushing the gunwale. The timber's chafing against my wound.

A jet of pain runs through me.

And I open my eyes.

And there below me is the water, just a hand's reach away. But my hands are nowhere near it. I got a ring bolt in one and a bollard thing in the other, and I'm clasping 'em tight. But my head's over the side of the boat and I'm looking down into that black face.

"You laughing at me, dungpot?"

The water gurgles against the side of the boat.

"You are laughing." I spit down into it. "Laughing at my fear."

Sound of an engine jerks my eyes back up.

The launch is moving again. Christ, Bigeyes, what am I doing? I should've been watching for this. And now I'm stuck out here. Least I'm lying down. But if they come this way, I'm plugged.

They don't.

Thank God. They're heading off down the river. Watch 'em go, chug, chug, chug. Yeah, go on, grinks. Wig it all the way to hell. They hit the bend, disappear round it, and they're gone.

I look back at the water below me.

Same squinty face.

"You're still laughing at me." I spit into it again. "Well, I don't care. Here, have some food."

I pull the plastic bag out of my pocket, reach down and let the water fill it. The apple cores and banana skin swim round inside like dronky fish. I let go of the bag and it slips from view. I snarl at the water.

"Thirsty, are you?"

I pull out the bottle of mineral water.

"Want some of this, claphead?"

It's almost full. I only had a couple of sips before I fell

asleep. I let it drop. It gives a little splash and then slips away too. And now it's just me again. Me and the black face laughing up. Like it doesn't give two bells if I live or die.

I pull out the knife, flick it open, stare down at the water again.

"If I could kill you, I would."

Another ripple on the surface. Another gurgle against the side of the hull. I let the knife fall. It stabs the black face and goes straight down. I feel the tears start again, pull myself back from the edge, stand up.

And see a new boat moving on the river.

27

CROUCH DOWN AGAIN, PEER OUT. A rowing boat, small, more of a dinghy. One person in it. Can't see who. Too dark. No splashing with the oars, just an even stroke. Whoever it is knows how to row. Ease back into the wheelhouse, still low, still peering out.

Dinghy's coming this way.

No question about it. No weaving about to check the other boats. This neb's heading for me. Least it's just one person. One against one if it bloods up. But now I can see who it is.

Bex.

Don't know if I'm pleased or angry. I want to get off this tub. But I don't want to spend time with that troll. Not after she lied about Jaz. She zipped me over too bad with that. And I won't forgive her.

But I suppose I can crack a few minutes with her if it gets me ashore.

Trouble is, I got a feeling it's going to be more than a few minutes. Cos the truth is, Bigeyes, I still haven't got any strength. Not enough to wig it anyway. And there's no way Bex is on her own. She's rowing out by herself but there's got to be others waiting on shore.

And I won't get away from them.

But never mind that now. First things first. Get off this tub. Get back to the shore. Then decide what to do. She's getting closer. Handling that dinghy like a pro. I'll give her that. Guess there's one thing she can do well, apart from lie.

She's just a short way off now. Stops rowing, spins the boat round so she's facing me, shouts over the water.

"Blade!"

Yeah, troll. Tell the whole world I'm here.

"Come out of the wheelhouse," she calls, "and go down the stern. It's easier to get in the dinghy from there."

I can't believe this dreg. She's just rowed straight out here and now she's popping her mouth for everyone to hear. She's not even looking round to check for trouble. I got to stop this before she does something worse.

I bustle out on deck, growl down at her.

"Don't make so much noise."

"There's nobody 'ere." She looks up at me like I'm a tick. "River's empty. Get down the stern." She nods toward it. "The back."

"I know where the stern is," I mutter.

She doesn't answer. She's already pulling toward it. We get there same time.

"Jump in," she says.

I stare down. Dinghy's bobbing like a ball. I'm not getting in that.

"What's wrong?" she says.

"Nothing."

"You're trembling."

I don't answer.

"It's no big deal," she says. "Water's calm."

It's not, Bigeyes. It was calm before but now it's bucking like hell. Don't shake your head. It's bucking like hell, okay?

140

"Just climb on the edge," she says, "and stick your bum on it. Then ease your feet down into the dinghy. I'll help you."

"No, you won't."

I climb onto the edge, sit down.

"I'll guide your feet," she says.

"Don't touch me."

I ease myself down, still clinging to the side of the motorboat. Bex grabs my feet before I can kick her hands away and steers them to the bottom of the dinghy.

"Let go of the motorboat and sit down," she says.

I slump onto the thwart in the stern of the dinghy.

"Jesus," she mumbles. "What a fuss."

"Just row."

She starts to row back toward the shore. I don't speak. I can't. I got nothing I want to say to Bex anyway but that's not it. I'm choked up to my brains with the water so close.

"You okay?" she says.

"Why shouldn't I be?"

"You're gripping the thwart like your life depends on it."

"Just row, okay? And shut your mouth."

She does one but not the other.

"Don't know why you're slagging me off. I ain't done you no harm."

"You lied about Jaz."

"And you never lied to me?" She stops rowing, fixes me. "You done nothing but lie."

"How do you know?"

"I just do." She glowers at me. "You saying I'm wrong?"

I shrug.

"You ain't told me nothing," she says. "Nothing much any-way. Nothing about them guys what's after you. Nothing

141

about who you is or what you done. And how much of what you have told me's true, eh? Shit all, I'm guessing."

I look away.

"Shit all," she says.

And she goes on rowing.

Yeah, I know, Bigeyes. She's right. But I still hate her. And I'm too tired to argue about it anymore. I just want to lie down, somewhere safe. But I reckon that's too much to hope for tonight. Still, as long as Bex keeps quiet for a bit.

But that's too much to hope for too.

"I come to get you cos of them guys in the launch."

I look back at her.

"We seen 'em," she says. "Me and Dig. We was on the shore. Coming to bring some more food. And check you out."

She's watching me close. Can't read her face. She's not angry anymore. I can tell that much. But I can't tell the rest. I think she wants me to trust her. Like I'm ever going to do that.

She's still watching me.

"Dig sent me to bring you in," she says. "He reckons them guys might come back cos they didn't finish checking all the boats. So we got to take you somewhere else tonight." She glances over her shoulder, then back at me. "Only we don't know where. Just know you can't stay on the boat."

"Whose is it?"

"Jojo's dad's. This dinghy's his too."

"Who's Jojo?"

"Xen's boyfriend."

"So that's two more people you told about me."

Bex shakes her head.

"Jojo just knows we're helping some kid. His dad don't know nothing."

I don't like it, Bigeyes. I don't like it one bit. But there's nothing I can do. And I'm feeling dizzy again, like the blacko's coming back.

"Blade?" says Bex.

"What?"

"You don't look too good."

"Thanks."

"Your forehead—"

"What about it?"

"Just looks . . ."

I reach up, feel the bandage. It's still on, underneath the woolly hat. But they're both wet.

"I know," I say. "Looks gross."

"Dig feels bad about it."

"Bit late for that now."

She doesn't answer. We're close to the shore and she's checking over her shoulder. I can see a figure over by the landing stage to the left. But it's not Dig. It's one of the trolls.

Xen.

Check round for the others. No sign of anyone. But I can see the van parked up the road. Same one Riff was driving. Bex is pulling toward the landing stage. I look at her.

"How come it's just you fetching me?"

"Cos the others ain't much good at rowing." She sniffs, wipes her nose on her sleeve, rows on. "And I am."

"How come?"

"I was born by the sea. And my bastard dad used to get me

to row him out to his sailing cruiser." She sniffs again. "Only he never wanted to do no sailing."

She goes quiet, looks away, looks back. And suddenly I read her face clear, like I can see everything she wants to say, but can't. I stare at her, swallow hard. I want to tell her I'm sorry. I want to tell her I get it. But she speaks first, in a quick, hard voice, like she wants to stop me.

"There's another reason it's just me."

"Yeah?"

"Dig says it don't look so suspicious."

I still want to speak. Say sorry. Cos I know where she's been, Bigeyes. Sort of. Wasn't the same for me. Different circumstances. But the same result. I look at her, open my mouth—but she glares at me and I know she doesn't want to hear.

Check round again. No other figures, no movement. Just Xen waiting on the landing stage, hands in her pockets.

"What time is it?" I say.

Bex isn't listening. She's checking over her shoulder again as she pulls in.

"Bex, what time is it?"

"Christ knows," she mutters. "Ten, eleven, whatever."

I look round again. Water, boats, shore. No sign of anyone, apart from Xen and us. But I'm telling you, Bigeyes, I can feel nebs everywhere. Grinks, porkers, God knows who else. And they're close. Don't ask me how I know.

Bex brings us alongside the landing stage, glances at me.

"You can stop clutching the thwart now."

28

XEN LOOKS DOWN, SPARKY FACE, sparky eyes, bit like Kat's only harder. Don't go for this troll. Don't trust her. And I'll tell you something, Bigeyes. I might be ill, might be weak, might be missing stuff, but there's one thing I can see.

She's no friend of Bex's. I can tell. And it's mutual. Look at 'em both. Gut flush, eyes ripping. But never mind that. Here's Dig leaning down. Didn't see him get out of the van, hit the landing stage. That scares me.

I don't mean seeing him. I mean not seeing him. I never used to miss stuff like that. But I didn't see him move, and here he is. And now I'm slotting something else, something about the two trolls. The way they're looking at him.

Okay, I get it. Probably Dig does too. Probably he likes it. But who gives two bells? Not me, Bigeyes. It's their problem. I'm too blasted to bother. All I want is to get off this effing water and crash somewhere. Never mind a snug. Just leave me in the van. I'm past caring.

"Get him out of the dinghy," says Dig.

Don't know how they sting it. I certainly don't help 'em. But somehow I'm up on the landing stage, and I'm standing, kind of, and Dig's half pulling, half carrying me to the van. And you know what?

I don't even mind that. Him touching me and all. I'm so wiped I hardly notice. I hear the back door of the van open, feel myself pushed in, hear the door close, and now it's dark. Someone's next to me. Don't know who.

Wish it was Jaz.

But it's Bex. I can see now. Twist my head round, peer toward the front. Dig's in the driver's seat, Xen next to him. And there's that look again. Hers on him. I don't clock Jojo's chances with her. But I'll tell you something else.

I don't clock hers on Dig either.

Cos one thing's bung-clear: Dig's got someone else now. Someone he had before. Someone who's now forgiven. There's no missing it. I lie down, murmur to Bex.

"You're back with Dig."

She doesn't answer. I close my eyes.

"Bex?"

"What?"

"You spoken to the police?"

"No."

"They're looking for you."

"They're looking for all of us," she says. "You, me and Jaz."

"But you and Jaz aren't missing anymore. You're back. So what did you tell the police? They must have been round asking questions."

"Ain't told 'em nothing. Kept out of the way when they come. Kept Jaz out of the way too."

"So they think you're still missing?"

"Yeah."

"And Jaz?"

"Yeah."

I don't like this, Bigeyes. What Bex does is her business. I know she's scared of the porkers cos she told me that once before. But Jaz is another matter. I hate the little kid getting mixed up in all this. But I can't think of any of that now.

Dig calls back.

"Pull the blanket over him."

Bex does what he says. It smells moldy but it's warm. Dig calls out again.

"Keep him out of sight. Keep him lying down."

I got no problem with that, Bigeyes. Cos I'm not moving. Dig starts the engine and we pull away. I feel Bex lean closer. But I keep my eyes shut.

"You got to stay down," she says.

I don't answer. She goes on.

"There's police everywhere. And other weirdos. Like them guys. You probably know who they are. But I suppose you ain't telling us."

I say nothing. I can feel the darkness wrapping me up. And it's plum.

"Shit!" says Dig suddenly.

"What?" says Bex.

"Police cars. And a motorbike."

I keep my eyes closed, pull the woolly hat down over 'em. Don't know why I'm not whammed about the crap outside. Maybe it's cos I know there's nothing I can do. I got no strength to fight or run. I'm stuck here and I'm cute about it for the moment. No decisions to make. It's Dig's gripe. He's spinning the wheel now and whisking us off down another street.

But he's soon muttering again.

"Bloody hell. More of the bastards."

He spins the wheel again and we drive on, cutting left, cutting right, cutting everywhere, and so it goes on, road after road, change after change, till I hear the groan of the brakes again. And the sound of Dig pounding the wheel.

"Christ, they're stopping the traffic now. I can see 'em up the road."

"How many's out there?" says Bex.

Xen gives a snort.

"You blind or something?"

Bex snaps back an answer.

"Course I ain't! But I weren't looking that way."

"Then turn your 'ead."

"I'm keeping an eye on Blade."

"What for? He's asleep, ain't he?"

"Dunno."

"Well, he ain't moved or done nothing for ages."

"Hey!" Dig snarls at 'em. "Stop the bickering. I got to think. Got to work out how to get round the police cars."

"Sorry, Dig," says Xen.

There's a silence. Goes on and on. Like none of 'em wants to break it. Cos none of 'em knows what to do. I call out.

"Cut left onto Adams Street. Take the little lane halfway down on the right. There's just enough room to get the van through. Then cut back down St. Stephen's Gardens and you'll be round the police."

More silence. Just the sound of the engine ticking over. Dig speaks.

"How come you know where we are?"

I don't answer.

"Eh?" he says. "You been lying there with that hat over your eyes since we left the river. I seen you in the mirror. You ain't moved once. And we changed roads like I don't know how many times."

Yeah, Diggy, wonder all you want. But if you knew the city like I do, you'd know it's a spit to keep a check on the roads you just took. All of 'em. Even with my eyes closed, even blasted like this. There wasn't a moment when I didn't know where we were.

I pull the hat farther down over my eyes.

"Cut left onto Adams Street. Do it now while you got a chance."

He doesn't argue. I hear the engine rev up, then we turn left and I feel us rumbling down Adams Street.

"Can't see no lane," he mutters.

"It's just past the deli."

"Can't see no deli," says Xen.

"It's farther down."

She sparks back at me.

"How do you know if you ain't looking?"

"I don't need to look. I can tell."

"You're weird."

"You're shit."

She makes a huffy noise but says no more. Nearby Bex gives a chuckle. I call out to Dig.

"You should be able to see the deli now."

"I got it."

"Be careful how you turn. It's narrow."

Sound of the van slowing down. He's giving the wall of the deli a wide berth to get into the lane. And now we're heading down it. I can feel the rumble of the wheels over the uneven surface. We reach the end and I feel him turn into St. Stephen's Gardens.

"You're right," he says after a moment. "We got round the police."

Clever boy, Digsy. Only it won't last, Bigeyes. Cos there'll be more. And the porkers are the nicest of the nebs out cruising tonight. Run my hand under the woolly hat, up over my forehead. The bandage and the hat both feel wet. But I don't think I'm bleeding anymore.

Just wish I had some energy, and my head straight again. But I got neither. Night's looking bleak, Bigeyes. Cos one thing's slick-sure: Dig's got no idea where to take me. He's rescued me—yeah, he's done that. Don't know why. Guilt probably, for hurting me, now that he's worked out I didn't kill Trixi.

But he's brained out on what to do with me.

And he's starting to panic.

He's got porkers chewing his ankles, and grinks, and me blobbed in his van. And he's got a conscience cos he plugged me with his knife. Poor clapper. Cos I'll tell you, Bigeyes, you don't want a conscience. Not if you want to stay alive. So he's in the grime.

He's driving down St. Stephen's Gardens and he's got no idea where to take me. Don't ask me how I know. There you go. We've reached the end of the road and he's stopped. I don't have to look out to see it. He's whipping his head to find a plan. But nothing's coming.

I call out again.

"Turn down Wisteria Drive, take the second right and the first left, and keep going till you reach the allotments."

Another silence, just the engine grumbling. I can feel 'em all watching. They're scared of me now, Bigeyes. Trust me. I know. So I got to be careful. Scared means dangerous with some nebs. And these nebs were dangerous already.

They might have helped me. But that only counts for so much.

I keep my eyes closed, lie still. Darkness feels warm. Engine revs up again. Not a word from Dig, but he's doing what I said. Down Wisteria Drive, second right, first left, and we're on our way to the allotments.

"Follow the road round," I say. "Keep the allotments on your right."

"Why don't you sit up?" says Xen. "Sit up and watch proper."

Hear that, Bigeyes? There's an edge in her voice. Sharper than it was before. I told you—she's scared. So she's dangerous again.

"I'm too tired to sit up," I say.

"Which way now?" calls Dig.

"Right at the fork. Then right again. It'll take you—"

"I know where it takes me." Dig gives a pause. "I live in this city, okay?"

And there's an edge in Dig's voice too.

29 GOT TO WATCH MY STEP, Bigeyes. Got to tread cute. They're not my friends. They're helping me for now but they're not my friends. I'm only here cos of Dig's conscience, but that's going to break soon. When it does, I'm smashed.

Close my eyes tight, try to think.

But it's hard. There's too much happening. And Dig's speeding up. I can hear it.

"Slow down," I call.

"It's an empty road," he answers.

"It's never an empty road."

"What's that supposed to mean?"

"Never mind. Just slow down."

He does, a bit. Not enough though. I know what's going on. He's losing his bottle. Yeah, Bigeyes, even Dig. I got to stop this somehow.

"You got to slow down," I say. "Got to drive normal."

"There's nobody in sight. We just left the houses behind. Who's to see us now?"

"You wouldn't want to know."

He goes quiet, slows down a bit more. Still going too fast but it's better than it was. Stupid dimp. I owe him but he's a dimp. He's met some of the grinks already, seen what they can do. He's probably guessed one of 'em plugged his sister. He's got to keep his cool or we're finished.

He calls back again.

"Which way?"

"Just keep driving down Baltimore Road."

He gives a kind of mutter, says no more. I got to watch this, Bigeyes. I'm drumming his brain big-time and he doesn't like it. Better sit up. It's me lying down and knowing where we are that's blitzing his head. I push myself upright.

"Hey," says Bex. "You're meant to be lying down."

I look at her. Don't know why but I don't hate her quite so much. She looks back. Something in her face I haven't seen before. Not what you'd call friendly. But not hostile either.

Can't say the same for Xen. She's twisted round in the front seat and she's skimming me with her eyes. I drill her back, keeping firm. She goes on watching for a bit, then flicks an eye at Bex and leans close to Dig.

"Dig?" she says.

"What?"

"He's sitting up."

"I noticed."

I catch Dig's glance in the mirror. Hard to tell if he's relieved or angry. He's certainly scared. Not as much as Xen but he's starting to choke up. I watch him in the mirror. He's still checking me out but he doesn't want to turn round proper.

"Another mile," I say.

"Then what?"

"You'll see a crossroads with a pub called—"

"The Queen Anne," he cuts in. "I know it."

"Go over the crossroads and there's a right turn just after it."

"And we go down there?"

Xen slants her eyes at him. She's been watching me again

but she's checking him out too. And there's something in her face, Bigeyes, something that wasn't there before. Don't know what it is. But she's looking at Dig different.

Looking at me different.

And then I get it. She's wondering where the power is. Cos she doesn't know anymore, and it's cranking her out. She hates me already but if this goes on much longer, she'll start hating Dig too. Maybe she does already.

Dig speaks again.

"You ain't answered my question."

"We don't turn right. We carry on. Past The Queen Anne, past the turning."

"Then why mention the pub?" he says. "Why mention the right turn?"

"Cos there's a little lane just past the turning." I keep my voice steady. "And you can miss it easy as sniff. So slow down when you get to the pub, and slow down again when you see the first right. The lane's just after it and it's tiny. If you don't watch close, you'll go past it."

He says no more, just drives on. Xen goes on watching me for a bit, then turns away. I lie down again, eyes open now. Bex is sitting over me like before. Hard to read her face, but it's not angry. I know that much. She reaches out a hand.

"Don't touch me," I say.

She pulls the hand back, turns her head away, murmurs.

"She keeps asking after you."

"Who?" I say.

But I know the answer, Bigeyes. You bet I do. Bex turns back.

"You know who I mean."

I picture Jaz's face. Christ, I wish she was here. I don't

mean with all this shit. The danger, the dronks, all that. I mean her and me somewhere else. A little room in a little snug, pictures on the wall, mobiles hanging from the ceiling, toys, books. Yeah, books. Lots of 'em. I wish we had all that.

I could make her trust me again. Maybe even like me. I know I could. Bex goes on.

"You scared her so bad that time. But after she stopped screaming, she started asking where you were. And she's kept on."

"Where's she now?"

"Somewhere safe."

"Well, you keep her there, all right? You just bloody keep her there."

Bex doesn't answer.

"Queen Anne ahead," calls Dig.

I sit up again, peer forward.

"Okay." I reach out and point. "See the right turn? Other side of the crossroads?"

"Yeah."

"Head for it. But slow down when you get near. Cos the lane's just past it."

He's still going too fast, Bigeyes, but I got no control over that. He'll drive how he wants. We rattle past the pub, over the crossroads and here's the right turn. Dig slows down at last, checking the side of the road.

"Can't see no lane," he mutters.

"Bit farther. You'll see some bushes and—"

"There!" says Bex.

She's moved forward and she's peering out with us. Xen glares at her for a moment, like she's guffed she didn't spot 'em herself. Bex takes no notice and points.

"There, Dig."

"I got it."

He checks round, turns into the lane. Leaves brush the van as we slip in.

"Bloody narrow," he grumbles. Glances round at me. "What is this place?"

"A private house."

"You serious?"

"Yeah. Drive on till we're out of sight of the road. It's only a little way. Lane bends just ahead."

He does as I say. I check behind, make sure we're cute.

"Okay, stop."

He stops, looks round. I check him over. And there it is again. Same thing in his face as Xen's got in hers. He's doing what she's doing. Wondering who's got the power. Cos he doesn't know anymore. And he's scared it might not be him.

He glances at Xen, Bex, me again. I got to play this smart, Bigeyes. Got to give him the power back somehow. Or make him think he's got it. Trouble is, he doesn't know what to do next. And I do. He scowls at me.

"What now?"

I nod to the left.

"Drive the van in among those trees."

"Off the lane?"

"Yeah. Hide the van. Case someone cuts in after us."

Like they could any moment, Bigeyes. Cos I'm telling you—that wasn't an empty road we just left behind. Dig might have thought it was but I know better. He turns off the lane, bumps the van over the grass and into the trees.

"Bit farther," I say.

"Shut your mouth." He glowers at me. "I'm doing it."

He drives round the biggest clump of trees, stops, turns off the engine. Silence falls like a fog. They're all looking at me, waiting.

"Now what?" says Dig.

I look back at him and suddenly I can't speak. You know why, Bigeyes? Cos I'm choked up about this bit. Choked twice over. First up, there's too many nebs died cos of me. And second, I don't like showing people my snugs. Not even when I'm desperate.

'Specially not Dig's kind of crew.

And this snug's special. Big old rambly house, set back down a twisty lane. Just one old gobbo in it, and he's away right now. I know that. I always check his desk diary when I'm there. Professor of philosophy. Lectures all over the world. One busy gobbo.

And I like him. He's kind of helpless. He might know all the clever crap but he can't cook, can't sort his clothes, can't fix the fence, and he definitely can't work the burglar alarm. It was different when his wife was there. She cracked all that stuff for him. I couldn't use the snug much when she was around.

But she died last year. And since then I've felt sorry for him, cos he's sad. Yeah, I like him a lot. Not that he knows that. He doesn't even know I exist. But he's a sweet old gobbo and I don't want Dig's trolls crabbing all over his stuff. And worse still . . .

Worse by far . . .

I don't want the grinks locking on to him.

I couldn't bear that, Bigeyes. I'm telling you.

"Well?" says Dig.

I stare out the window. Just a short walk. That's all it is.

A trig up the lane and there's a big, warm house waiting with no one in it. And he won't be back for a week.

I got to do it, Bigeyes. I got to rest so bad. And somehow I got to trust these dronks. But all I can see in my head is the old prof's face peering at me. I peer back. He doesn't look happy. I don't suppose I do either.

I'm sorry, old gobbo. I'm really sorry.

His face doesn't change. I look back at Dig and the trolls.

"Come with me," I say.

30

OUT OF THE VAN, up the lane, round the back of the house. I'm still seeing that old prof's face in my head. Try to block it out, fix my rap on what I got to do. But it's hard. I'm so bombed out I'm hardly thinking.

Just know I got to get inside and rest.

And somehow try and stop these dregs from grilling the old gobbo's house. Cos they will, Bigeyes. There's no way they'll leave it alone. This place won't be a snug after to-night. It's the last time I'll ever use it.

But I suppose I got no choice.

It's let 'em in or go somewhere else. And we got nowhere else as good as this right now. Nowhere I can think of any-way. And Dig's crew haven't come up with anything better.

"You sure about this?" says Dig.

I stop, look back at him. He's watching me in the dark-ness, eyes like bullets. Xen and Bex are standing either side of him, watching too. Watching me. I shrug.

"Yeah."

"Nobody 'ere?" says Dig.

"It's empty."

"There's a light on upstairs."

There always is, Bigeyes. There'll be one on downstairs too, round the other side of the house. The lounge. The curtains'll be drawn and the radio'll be on. It's just the prof trying to tell the world he's in when he's out.

Bless him.

"It's empty," I say.

I don't wait for an answer, just walk on round the building. Got to check things out like I always do, just in case I missed something. But it's all cute. Car's gone, garage empty. Upstairs light's the same as it always is.

The landing light.

Walk farther round. Close to the lounge window now.

"I can hear something," says Xen. "A radio."

"There's no one in," I say.

A hand grips my shoulder. It's Dig. I don't need to turn. But I do, slow. I stare into his eyes and there's that power thing again. He hates this, not knowing if he's in control. I got to tread soft, Bigeyes. I want to get inside, want to rest. But I got to work with this crew. I mustn't fizz 'em too much. 'Specially Dig.

He leans closer.

"How come you know about this place?"

I give another shrug.

"I know the guy who lives here. He's got his radio plugged into the wall socket by the television. And when he goes out, he leaves it on permanent. Keeps the curtains drawn and the light on."

"What about that light upstairs?"

"It's the landing light. He leaves that on too."

Dig's eyes move over me. I can almost feel 'em scratching me.

"You better be right," he mutters.

I don't answer.

"So which way in?" he says. "Break a window?"

Yeah, Bigeyes, like I'd do that. Even if I needed to. Which I don't. I shake my head.

"Much easier."

I walk on, past the front door, still checking cute. I can feel 'em fuming up behind me. Like they don't know how important this is, watching, knowing, making sure. Yeah, the prof's out. I can feel that. Even blasted in my head I can feel that.

But I still check. I still make sure.

Cos I'm good.

"Now where are you going?" says Dig.

"Round the back of the house."

"We just been there."

Jesus, Bigeyes, see what I'm dealing with? I don't answer. Can't talk to this dronk. If he can't see why we got to check things thorough, I can't help him. Round to the back door, under the little porch, stop.

"Now what?" says Dig.

I look round. I was hoping I might be able to do this without 'em seeing. But it's no good. They're fixing me cute, all three. Reach up, feel round the inside of the porch, where the roof meets the side panel. And there it is.

The key.

Dig's watching, narrowed eyes.

"How'd you know he keeps it there?"

He doesn't keep it there, Bigeyes. This is a copy the prof doesn't know about. He keeps his own key under the plant pot over there. Yeah, Bigeyes, some nebs really are that stupid. This is one I made when I first started coming here. Case the old gobbo ever got wise enough to put the other one somewhere else.

"Never mind," I say.

I open the door, let us in. Bex and Xen slip in ahead. Dig nods me through and comes after, then closes the door. From the lounge comes the sound of the radio. Xen and Bex look scared, like they're still not sure the house is empty.

"Come on," I say.

I lead 'em through to the lounge, show 'em there's no one in there, then take 'em through the rest of the house. But I'm hating this, Bigeyes. When I'm here on my own, it's okay. I treat the place good, like I do all my snugs.

And I like this one. I always did. I like the photos everywhere, of him and his wife. All the awards he's won, and the ornaments in the cabinets. And the books. Yeah, the books. He must have thousands.

Big stuff too, heavy stuff. Philosophy and all. Can't crack most of it. But I like reading it. Don't know why. Maybe it was that Nietzsche book I told you about. The one I read in that other snug. Maybe that's what did it.

I kind of like this stuff now. Doesn't beat stories. Nothing could. But it stings my head and I'm cute about that. Yeah, I like this snug. But not with Dig and the trolls here. With them around I feel like I'm pissing on the old man's face.

And when the rest of the crew get here, it'll be worse. Cos they're on their way, Bigeyes. Trust me. Xen's on her mobile already, talking to Riff. She sees me watching and takes off to another room.

"I'll check if there's any food," says Bex.

And she goes.

I look at Dig. We're standing in the hall again and he's close. He's been like that all the time we were going through the rooms. I check out his eyes. They're hard like before, hard and wary. He's still got his conscience. But only just.

He nods me toward the lounge.

I walk through ahead of him, throw myself down on the sofa. I just want to curl up and sleep. I'm not ready to talk, not yet. I want to rest first, think first. But Dig's got stuff in his head. There'll be no rest till we've sorted that.

He leans down, turns off the radio, sits in the armchair, pulls it closer. Xen comes back. She's stopped talking on the phone but she's texting someone. Sits on the floor, glances at me, then at Dig. His face doesn't change. She goes back to her texting. Bex appears in the doorway.

"No food. Nothing."

I could have told her that, Bigeyes. You know why? Cos there's never any food in the house now. The old prof's fallen apart since his missus died. That's another reason why I feel sorry for him. He used to eat real good when she was around.

And so did I.

"Make some tea," says Dig. "There's got to be some of that."

"There ain't," says Bex. "Instant coffee, that's all. No milk."

"Then make that, for Christ's sake." Dig glares at her. "And when we got our coffee . . ." He fixes his gaze back on me. "We'll decide what we're going to do about Blade."

There's a silence. Just the sound of Xen texting. Then that stops. I stare back at Dig. I got to play this right.

"There's nothing you got to do about me," I say.

He doesn't answer, just watches. Xen jets a glance at him, but he doesn't notice. He's still watching my face. I'm watching both of 'em. And Bex, still standing in the doorway.

"There's nothing you got to do about me," I say. "I just got to rest. And then we can split."

Dig shakes his head.

"We ain't going to split just yet."

"Why not?"

"Cos you got stuff to explain."

"Yeah?"

"Yeah."

I watch him. He watches me.

"Like what?" I say eventually.

He leans closer.

"Well, for starters," he says, "you can tell us about them marks on your back."

31

IT'S TAKEN 'EM LONG ENOUGH TO ASK. The trolls would have seen the marks that time they stripped me on the towpath. But nobody spoke up. Not even Bex. And she had plenty of chances later.

So did you, Bigeyes.

But maybe you were all scared. Cos wounds freak people out. 'Specially wounds like mine.

"Well?" says Dig.

I'm not telling him, Bigeyes. Or you. Forget it, okay? It's like I said right in the beginning—I choose what I say and what I don't. You can choose whether to stay or wig it somewhere else.

My secret.

Not yours.

"I'm waiting," says Dig.

He's watching cute. So's Xen. So's Bex. She still hasn't moved from the doorway. I glance at her.

"Thought you were making coffee."

"Don't change the subject," says Dig.

I look back at him.

"I'm not," I say. "The subject's coffee. When that's here, we'll talk."

I hold his eyes, drill him. He doesn't like this. He's not used to it. Maybe he can see something I once was, something that's still left from the past. Maybe he doesn't know it's gone. And that's fine by me. I need him like this. Moment he knows he's stronger than me, I'm done.

He drills me back, hard as he can, but it's no good. He wavers first. Tries to cover it by flicking his gaze at Bex.

"Coffee," he snaps. "Make it quick."

She goes. And we wait.

Silence. A long silence. Just the sound of the kettle heating up in the kitchen and Bex hunting for cups. Dig and Xen watch. And I watch back. And we go on waiting. Bex comes back eventually, holding a tray with four cups on it.

"I found some sugar," she says.

"Nobody wants any," says Dig.

She doesn't answer, just puts the tray down. Nobody moves. She glances round, takes a cup in each hand, holds 'em out to Dig and Xen. Neither take any notice.

"I'll have one," I say.

She holds one of the cups out for me. I take it and put it on the floor. She keeps the other one herself and slumps with it in the chair by the television. The other two cups sit on the tray, untouched.

"I'm waiting," says Dig.

I shake my head.

"You first."

"About what?"

"About everything."

He reaches out, picks up a cup of coffee, blows off the steam.

"Everything's a lot of things," he drawls.

"You better get started then."

He watches me over the rim of the cup. I wait. He'll talk first. He's holding out as long as he can but he'll talk first.

Don't ask me how I know. He takes a sip, then suddenly starts.

"We thought you killed Trixi. Or Bex killed her. Or you both did. 'Specially when the girls saw you trying to get Jaz away. Police turned up, asking questions. Tammy told 'em all about you. I didn't want her to. I wanted you for myself."

I reach up, feel the wound in my head. It's hurting again. But it's dry.

Dig watches, goes on.

"So when them other guys showed up, it seemed like a better option."

"Paddy," I say quietly.

"Yeah." Dig takes another sip of coffee. "And his mates."

I shake my head.

"And you believed 'em."

"I still believe 'em."

"What?"

"I still believe 'em." Dig gives a little smile, but it quickly goes. "Not about you killing Trixi like they said. I did then but I don't now. But I believe 'em about the other stuff."

"What other stuff?"

"About you being a killer."

I feel Xen stiffen on the floor.

"Cos you are," says Dig. "Ain't you?"

I don't answer. He waits, like to give me space. I say nothing, let him fill it instead.

"I was happy to believe Paddy," he goes on. "So when he said him and his mates was after you for other murders, it seemed like a good idea to work together. Riff kept in touch with 'em. And one way and another, we found you."

"Yeah." I feel my wound again. "You found me."

He says nothing. He's watching close, not my eyes this time, but my hand on the bandage. And I can see it in his face, Bigeyes, bung-clear. He's stopped caring. No messing. Conscience is wiped now.

"So what changed everything?" I say.

"We threw you out of the *Sally Rose* and kicked Bex out an' all, cos we didn't want her no more. She can tell you the next bit."

I look at Bex. She's like Xen, sitting rigid.

"I saw them guys," she says. "They was following you to the warehouse. And then I saw this old woman. I recognized her from the bungalow. But I was too freaked out to think much. I just told her we got to do something. But then I panicked and ran off."

Xen gives a snort. Dig rounds on her.

"Don't assume you'd have done no better."

"I would have."

"I don't think so."

She gives him a baleful stare. He takes no notice, gives Bex a nod.

"Get on with it."

Bex looks at me.

"I was running off," she says, "running like shit. I'm way down the path and then I hear these gunshots. Two of 'em. Bang! Bang! Scared the crap out of me. I wanted to run on but I stopped and hid. There was this upturned dinghy just off the path. Wreck of a thing. I crouched down behind that. And I'm crying cos I think you're dead. And then . . . I know I got to go back. Find out what's happened. Do something. So I starts to run back—"

"See?" Dig swivels back to Xen. "You wouldn't have done that."

"I would."

"You wouldn't. You'd have pissed off out of it."

Xen doesn't answer, just scowls. This is bad, Bigeyes. I'm telling you. He doesn't need to whip Xen over like this. She's angry enough already. He'll only make it worse. But there's nothing I can do about it. This is about the three of 'em. And I'm not part of that.

He's looking back at me now.

"So Bex gets back where she was," he says, "and finds the police hanging around, and an ambulance taking you off to the hospital. Comes back to the *Sally Rose* and tells us what's happened. And next day we hear about Paddy."

"Being caught?" I say.

Dig shakes his head.

"Being dead."

32

SHIT, BIGEYES, HE'S SMACKED ME cold with this one. I knew about the porkers getting Paddy. The grunt told me when I was lying outside the warehouse. But I didn't see this coming.

Dig drinks the rest of his coffee, puts down the cup.

"It was on the news," he goes on. "About this guy being taken in by the police. Nothing about his name but it was obvious from the details they meant Paddy. And they was going on about how there was forensic evidence linking him and Trixi. Enough to know he was in the bungalow. Enough to know it wasn't you or Bex done my sister."

He glances at Xen.

"Enough for me anyway," he adds.

She turns her head away.

"But how'd he die?" I say.

Dig looks back at me.

"Result of a previous injury, the news said. Seems someone hit him with a cricket bat. Don't ask me how they knew it was a cricket bat. I don't suppose Paddy told 'em. But who cares? They got the forensic evidence. So I knew it wasn't you killed Trix."

He watches me, hard.

"Must have whopped Paddy real good," he murmurs. "Whoever had that cricket bat."

I don't answer. He waits a bit longer but I stay quiet. He goes on, still watching.

"So there's me starting to feel bad about what I done to your head. But I ain't got no time to think cos suddenly you gone missing again. It's all over the bloody news. You've broken out of the hospital and there's been more murders. And now we're in the shit too."

He leans closer.

"Cos the police is back asking stuff. And more of them guys. Not Paddy's crew. Other guys, guys we never seen before. Smooth bastards. Never come when the police is there, always some other time. Checking me out, checking the girls, checking Riff. Every time we look round, there's someone hanging close."

He pulls out the big knife, looks it over.

"They ain't never no trouble. It's all matey-matey. How's it going, Dig? All right, Dig? Seen that boy anywhere, Dig? Keep in touch, mate." Dig sniffs. "But I'm not stupid. So me and Riff and the girls talk. We agree to take Bex back . . ." He throws another glance at Xen, then fixes me again. "And help you."

Yeah, right. Hear that, Bigeyes? He almost spat out the last bit. Like he couldn't bear to say it. But I guess I can't be choosy. Fact is I'm here cos he went and got me. He didn't have to like it. He just had to do it. And he did. So I should be grateful.

Can't quite work out why I'm not.

Maybe it's cos I know that whatever he's done, he still hates me as much as I hate him. In which case, the sooner this game's over, the better for both of us. No more pretend. I watch him for a moment, wait for him to speak. He's got more to say. Not much, but I want to hear it.

"So we goes looking for you," he says. "Some mate of Trixi's tells us he's seen you on the north side. Says you was riding a bike. Riff takes the van that way while I check out other places on the motorbike. No sign. Then we gets another message. Someone Sash knows thinks he saw you. So we goes on looking."

Dig glances down, fingers the knife.

"Only there's others looking too."

Glances up again, straight at me.

"You know who I mean."

Yeah, Bigeyes, I know who he means. And he's not talking about the porkers. I'm thinking back to the lane. The dark little lane and my dark little dream of safety. How dimpy was that, Bigeyes? Eh? Must have been off my head to think I could get away. I'm seeing 'em again now, the figures crowding round in the night.

But I'm still alive. And I'm here. Cos of this guy in front of me. Whatever else I think of him, I owe him.

"Thanks," I say.

Dig looks at me quizzical.

"For helping me," I add.

He gives a sort of laugh.

"Long time coming," he mutters. He fingers the knife again. "But if you mean it, I'll take it."

"I mean it."

He glances at Bex, Xen, Bex again. I check out the trolls. Xen's looking down, meeting nobody's eyes, body all tight. Bex looks wary—of Xen, me, Dig, everything. Dig fixes me again.

"So I got you away and we put you on the motorboat. Didn't know what else to do. Couldn't use none of our places

172

cos them guys keep showing up, and the police. So we thought of the boat. But then we saw 'em checking out the moorings in that launch. So we come and got you. And now we're here."

"Thanks," I say again.

We watch each other in silence. I wait for Dig to break it.

"So," he says, "them marks on your back . . ."

"What about 'em?"

"Going to show me?"

"No."

His face hardens.

"The girls told me they was pretty spectacular."

"So?"

"So I reckon you owe me a look."

"I don't owe anyone a look."

His eyes run over me. I'm watching him cute, Bigeyes. Yeah, I know. You're thinking show him and have done. But that's cos you want to look at 'em too, right? Well, you can't, and he can't. I don't care what I owe him.

He's not seeing 'em. Unless he forces me. And he might try. He might just try. He leans back, stroking the knife, then speaks, low voice.

"So what do you owe me?"

"I said thanks."

"That's it? Thanks?"

"Yeah."

"Blade," says Bex.

I glance at her. She's got a pleading look in her face. Never seen it there before. Makes her look vulnerable. Don't know what I feel. She speaks again.

"You got to tell us about them guys. Who they is."

"You don't want to know 'em."

"How come they're after you? What you done to 'em?"

Nothing, Bigeyes. Before you ask. They're not the ones I've hurt. It's the nebs who've sent 'em that's the problem. They're the ones who really want me.

"I can't tell you about 'em," I say. "I got some enemies, okay?"

"More than some," says Dig. "I saw 'em crowding round you."

"And there's more coming." I fix my eyes on him. "Listen. You don't want to make this your problem. You've helped me. I'm grateful. But let it go. And let me go."

Dig looks down at the knife, runs a finger along the blade.

"And where will you go?" He looks up. "Eh? Going to tell me that much?"

"Away," I answer. "Somewhere far, somewhere safe."

"Is there such a place?"

I don't answer. Cos I don't know.

Dig puts the knife away. Xen's mobile starts to ring. She pulls it out.

"Yeah?"

We watch her in silence, waiting.

"It's a little lane," she says. "Bushes and stuff. You got it? Okay."

She rings off, looks round at us.

"They're 'ere."

33

XEN GOES TO THE FRONT DOOR to let 'em in. Riff comes first, eyes darting. What a surprise. I'll tell you what he's doing, Bigeyes. And I'll tell you what he's not doing. He's not checking for trouble. He's checking to see what he can cream.

I got that old prof's face in my head again. I'm sorry, old gobbo. I didn't want to bring these dregs into your house. But I just didn't know what else to do. Please don't be angry with me.

Kat and Tammy come next, then Sash.

Carrying Jaz in her arms.

"Jesus!" says Dig. "What you bring the kid for?"

"She won't sleep without Bex," says Sash.

"You was meant to stay behind and look after her. Not bring her here."

Tammy thrusts her face in front of Dig's.

"You deaf or something? Sash just said. Jaz won't sleep without Bex. And you know it. We found that out day one, remember?"

Dig doesn't answer. Jaz starts to whimper, reaches for Bex. I feel kind of weird, Bigeyes. Maybe it's cos I want her to reach for me. But she hasn't even looked at me. She's just staring at Bex.

"Put her down," says Bex. "She's knackered."

"Ain't slept, that's why," says Sash.

"Then put her down."

Sash puts Jaz down. Bex gives a smile.

"Come here, Fairybell."

Jaz runs into her arms, buries her face.

"There you go," says Bex, stroking her head. "All right now."

Jaz goes on whimpering. I look round at the others. They're all watching Dig.

"So what's going on?" says Riff.

"Me and Blade have had a little talk," says Dig.

He glances at Xen and Bex. Bex doesn't notice. She's snuggling Jaz, kissing the girl's hair. Xen just looks away. Dig watches her for a moment, then turns back to face me.

"We've had a little talk," he goes on. "Only I done most of the talking. Blade here don't choose to say much."

He drills me with his eyes.

"But I reckon we're quits now. Him and me."

He's waiting, Bigeyes. Waiting for something back. Fair enough. Can't argue with that. He slashed my head. But he got me away from the grinks. I give him a nod, a small one. But he sees it.

"So what you brung us 'ere for?" says Tammy.

Dig turns to her.

"To get Blade away."

"You what?"

"To get him away."

"What for?" Tammy stares at him. "We done enough for this shithead, ain't we?"

"No, we ain't."

"Why not?"

"Cos I say so." Dig fixes her hard for a moment. "We got him this far. We're going to finish it proper. Nice and tidy. So listen. We rest for a few hours. Cos we're all tired. And just before dawn we drive him out of the city."

"I don't like it," says Tammy.

"Nor me," says Sash.

"Well, I don't care," says Dig. "That's what we're doing."

"But them guys is all over the place," says Sash. "And the police."

"It's just to get him away." Dig pauses. "We go at the quiet time, just before dawn. Two vans, five minutes apart, different routes. One as a decoy. The other one to get him out of the city. I'll take that one. Drop him where he wants and that's it. All done."

He glances at me. And I nod again.

Yeah, that's it. All done.

For you lot anyway.

There's no more argument, even from Tammy. But she's not happy. I can tell. Nor are the others. They look blown out. And you can't blame 'em, Bigeyes. There's that many grinks in the city now, it's dangerous for everybody.

Dig checks his watch.

"Half past midnight. Rest up for a few hours. I'll call you when we're leaving."

We split. Or rather they do. I'm staying on the sofa. No point moving. I won't sleep anyway. I'm bombed out but I know I won't sleep, not while I'm still here.

I got to get out of the city, Bigeyes. Maybe then I'll sleep. But first I got to find a new place and play dead all over again. And play it better this time. Make sure the grinks don't find me.

And somehow stop Dig and his crew from getting hurt too. Cos I don't want that to happen. They've helped me,

Bigeyes. I don't like 'em, and they don't like me, but they've kept me alive and I owe 'em. And there's something even more important. Much more.

Jaz.

I got to keep her safe at all costs.

Check her out, Bigeyes. She's falling asleep in Bex's arms. Hasn't glanced at me once since she came in. Just went straight for Bex. I guess that's fair. Long as the kid's okay, doesn't matter what I feel.

Except to me.

It matters to me.

Dig's still sitting in the armchair. Xen's wigged it upstairs, so have Tammy and Sash. I can hear 'em moving about. I feel guilty for the old prof again. I hate the thought of these dronks tramping over his gear.

Riff and Kat are still hanging about. Kat's blasted and wants to sleep. Anyone can see that. But Riff's still picking stuff up, checking it over.

"Riff," says Dig. "We got to sleep."

Riff looks round at him, then at Kat. Puts down the little vase he was holding, gives her a wink.

"Come on, then," he smirks.

Yeah, dungpot, we know what you want. But he's out of luck, Bigeyes. Cop a glint at Kat's face. See that? It's a big, big no. She sees me looking, gives a flinty little smile, walks out of the room and up the stairs. Riff follows, checking ornaments as he goes.

"Blade."

Dig's watching me again.

"Yeah?" I say.

"Me and Bex on the sofa."

It's not a request. I can hear it in his voice. And you know what, Bigeyes? I don't give two bells. He wants his power back. Well, he can have it. He's helping me one last time. I owe him the sofa. I stand up, look over at Bex.

She's stood up too, holding Jaz in her arms, fast asleep now. She carries the kid over, sits down with her on the sofa. Dig comes over too, sits down in my place.

"You don't got to go, Blade," says Bex. "Have Dig's armchair."

Yeah, Bigeyes. Cute thought, eh? I don't even have to look at Dig's face to know how much he likes the idea. Well, he'll have to deal with it. I'm sitting in the armchair. Not cos I want to give 'em trouble. But cos . . . well . . . if you really want to know . . .

I want to be near Jaz.

I don't want to let her out of my sight. Cos this is the last night I'll ever see her. And I want as much of her as I can get, even asleep. Cos you know what? I'm going to have to live off that memory soon.

Slump down in the armchair, close my eyes.

Someone turns off the light. I don't bother to check who. Dig probably. When I peep out again, it's all dark. Dig and Bex are curled up on the sofa, Jaz nestled under Bex's arm. They look kind of sweet. Can't say they don't.

And I feel weird again.

But then somehow I sleep. Didn't expect to but it comes over me like warm rain. And a dream comes with it. I'm dreaming of Becky, sweet Becky who died. I can see her face clear as the sun. And she's talking to me.

Only I can't make out the words.

Then I get 'em.

"Blade," she's murmuring.

And that's it. My name.

"Blade, Blade . . ."

That's all she's saying. And now there's a hand on my shoulder, and it's rocking me gentle. And the name's coming again.

"Blade, Blade."

And that's gentle too. So I open my eyes. And here's the room back again, and it's dark like before. Bex and Dig have left the sofa but I know where they've gone. I can hear 'em upstairs. In the old prof's bedroom. The one he shared with his wife.

The hand rocks my shoulder again. The voice repeats my name.

"Blade," it says.

"Jaz," I answer.

And she climbs up into my arms and I hold her tight.

34

SHE DOESN'T TALK. But she's awake, she's aware of me. She's looking up at me with sleepy eyes. I look down into 'em, try and smile. Don't know if I manage it. But I speak. I manage that, just.

"All right, baby?"

I sound like a dimp. I'm embarrassed by my own voice. She doesn't answer. Closes her eyes, opens 'em again. She's only half awake. I pull her closer. She doesn't resist. And nor do I. Didn't know I could hold someone close and not feel bad.

But I'm cute about this. Touching, being touched. Cos she's touching me too. Her little hand's moving, just a bit, over my arm. Stops, moves, stops. Now it's resting, still on my arm. She wriggles a bit, closes her eyes again.

More sounds upstairs. Not loud but enough for me to clap 'em. Just hope Jaz can't. They're not the sounds a kid should hear. But it's okay. I think she's dropping off again. I'm wrong.

"Blade," she murmurs.

I look down at her. She's peering up at me again, same sleepy eyes. I lean closer, whisper.

"Do you want to hear a story?"

She gives a little moan. I think that's a yes.

"It's a great story," I say. "About this little girl."

"What's she called?"

"Jaz."

"That's my name."

"I know, baby. Weird, yeah?"

"Hm."

"Do you want to know what happens to her?"

"Hm."

"She's sitting by this rabbit hole one day and guess who she sees coming along?"

"Bunny."

"Yeah, it's Mr. Bunny."

"Where's he going?"

"He's just coming back from the shops."

"Where's Mrs. Bunny?"

"She's down the bunny hole. She's angry with him."

"What for?"

"Cos he's late. She sent him out ages ago to get some bread but he met a friend in the shop and that was it. No getting away for hours."

"Why?"

"Cos he's a chatterbox."

"Mr. Bunny?"

"Yeah. Yak yak yak. Talks forever."

Jaz's eyes widen.

"Forever?"

"Well, he stops sometimes to have a rest. But pretty soon he starts all over again."

"Is Mrs. Bunny very angry with him?"

"Very very very angry. And she's going to be even more angry when he gets back inside the bunny hole."

"Why?"

"Cos he forgot the bread."

"Where is it?"

"He left it back in the shop. But don't worry, cos Jaz comes to the rescue."

Her eyes are closing again. More sounds upstairs. But they're easing off a bit. And now it's all quiet. Just the sound of Jaz breathing, tucked into my chest. She looks so beautiful, Bigeyes, like a little flower. Makes me think of Becky again.

"You asleep, baby?" I murmur.

No answer. The breathing goes on. I stare round the room, whisper into the darkness.

"Too many stories, Jaz. Too many to tell. And they all seem to hurt."

I look down at her again.

"But I'll make sure yours has got a happy ending." I stroke her hair. "I'll finish it when you wake up."

She goes on sleeping. I'm glad. I want her to sleep. Even if I can't. I breathe out, listen. House is quiet now. Not a sound anywhere. Even Jaz's breathing's gone silent. Check round. Behind me's the old prof's radio and next to it the little lights of the electric clock.

Five past two.

I reach out, switch the radio on, volume down as low as I can manage. Out comes a voice, faint but clear: some newsy woman.

". . . but the boy is still at large. There have been unconfirmed reports of him in different parts of the city, including one alleged sighting close to the house in which Mrs. Turner was murdered. The area has been cordoned off and police are appealing for witnesses . . ."

I look down at Jaz again. No change. Eyes closed, body still. She's sleeping deeper than ever. The newsy woman's voice goes on but I'm not really listening. I know what the porkers know, and what they don't. But then I hear something—and stiffen.

". . . an elderly woman, calling herself Lily . . ."

Christ, Bigeyes. They're talking about Mary.

Another voice, some gobbo reporter.

"Not really, Joanna. At this stage the police are simply saying they're anxious to interview the lady. She apparently found the boy when he was lying injured outside the warehouse, accompanied him to the hospital and spoke to him when he came round after his operation. She's not been seen since and though the police took a statement from her at the time of the injury, it now appears that she gave a false name and address. To complicate matters further, a witness has come forward and reported seeing someone matching this woman's description close to the bungalow where the teenager Trixi Kenton was killed."

I turn off the radio. And darkness fills my head.

What's happened to me, Bigeyes? Has my brain stopped working? Why wasn't I ready for this? Cos I've been thinking of Jaz and only Jaz, that's why. Wanting her to be all right. And that's cute. That's how it should be. But what about Mary?

Why didn't I look out for her?

Do you crack what I'm saying? This is bad, Bigeyes. I should have told her to get away. She can't stay here, not in this city. The porkers want her but they're not the grime. Even if they find her, they won't be able to protect her. The grinks'll want her more.

They've met her twice already. The old girl with the gun. They'll know all about that. So why's she still alive? Cos maybe they didn't connect her first go. They maybe just thought here's some old bird with a bit of spit and she's looking out for some kid.

And that's how it was.

Only now the porkers have blown that open. It's on the news. Everything about that report says Mary and me are linked up. Everything about it says she might know something. The porkers want to talk to her about it.

But the grinks'll want to talk to her even more.

She's in deep shit here, Bigeyes. And she doesn't know it. She's got to get out of the city, tonight, in the dark. Or go to ground big-time, then wig it when she can. Before they find her.

I might be too late already.

Check the clock again. Nearly quarter past two. I got a couple of hours before Dig cranks us up. Can't ring Mary from here. That'll get the nebs at the pub involved. I got to tell her—and just her. And I got to do it now.

I look down at Jaz. Still sleeping in my arms.

"Beautiful girl," I whisper.

I ease up from the chair, keeping her tight. She shifts a bit, wriggles in my arms, settles again. I carry her over to the sofa, put her softly down, cushion under her head. She goes on sleeping.

Like she could forever.

I kneel down, move close again.

"Don't wake up, baby," I murmur.

She doesn't. She just lies there, in the silence, in the darkness.

"I'll come back for you," I whisper. "I promise I will. I know I left you once before and didn't come back. But I will this time. No matter what happens, I'll come back and finish your story. And say good-bye."

I stand up again. But I'm still looking down. I can't take my eyes from her, Bigeyes. I can't do it. But I got to. Got to make myself. For Mary's sake. I reach out a hand. I want to touch her again. Once more. Just a little touch. But she moves, turns over, pushes her face into the cushion.

And I pull my hand back.

It's now, Bigeyes. It's got to be now.

And I head for the door.

35

INTO THE HALL, SOFT, SLOW, listening cute. No sound anywhere in the house. Nothing from the old prof's bedroom. Nothing from anywhere else. I could be in an empty snug.

Stop at the back door, listen again.

Still quiet. Just hope they're all sleeping, but I don't know if I'll be that lucky. I wouldn't sleep if I was them. Not if I knew what's sniffing after us. Push open the back door, slip out, close it soft.

Tiny click but not much. Listen again, then round the side of the house, down the lane, off into the trees. Two vans parked together. And here's the good news.

No fuss over keys. Dig left his in the ignition. Didn't think I spotted that, did you, Bigeyes? Well, I did. I saw him. Stupid tick. He thinks we're all comfy here, off the road, out of sight. So he didn't bother with the keys.

Bad news is the van's only got a drip of gas.

I spotted that too.

Riff's motor's probably got more but I'm not sneaking round the house trying to cream the keys off him. So we're taking Dig's van. Let's just hope the engine doesn't wake everybody up.

Jump in, close the door, check the gas gauge.

See what I mean? Quarter tank. He should have juiced up before the crap flew, but there you go. That's his business.

Just got to pray we get there and back. I got no money to buy gas and wouldn't dare stop at a garage if I had.

Let's get this over with.

Check round, turn the key. Engine fires straight off. Let it tick over till it chums up. I'm not revving loud case they hear. Check over there, Bigeyes, through the trees. You can just see part of the house. Any lights going on?

I can't see any.

Let's go.

Reverse gear, back to the apple tree, twist round, into the lane, down to the road. Stop, check both ways. No headlights either side, nothing in my mirror from the direction of the house. I'm half expecting Dig and the others to come running.

But they're not. I think we've done it, Bigeyes. They're sleeping on. I hope they don't stop. They're safer sleeping. Safer for everyone, including themselves. Come on. We got to move.

Left into the road and off. Getting really scared now, Bigeyes. I tell you, I'm hating this—heading back into the city. Cos that's where the grinks are. Or most of 'em. They'll be out this way too but the city'll be crawling with 'em.

Least we're heading for South Street. It's not far off the center but it's kind of a quiet little road and I might just be able to park out of sight and slip down to The Crown without anyone noticing.

I've already thought of a way into the pub.

That's where knowing the city helps. But let's get there first. If the porkers or grinks spot me driving the van, we won't even make it to The Crown. And we're starting to pick up traffic now.

Slow traffic.

Scary traffic.

Who drives anywhere this time of the morning? Sleepy nebs, drunken nebs, that's what you're thinking. Nebs going home, nebs going away. And you'd be right. But I don't see any of 'em. I just see danger.

In every car.

More traffic, porkers now, two cars and a motorbike coming the other way. They slip past. Drive on, check the mirror. They haven't stopped. Left onto Western Avenue, down to the end, right onto Sion Way.

More porkers, a van this time, parked just ahead, same side of the road. Got to drive past it, no way out. Some policeman standing on the sidewalk, talking to a gobbo.

But it's the gobbo in trouble, not me. He's waving his arms about, yelling. Policeman doesn't look fazed, and he doesn't check me out either. Drive on past, turn down Madeira Drive. Now it gets interesting.

Two more cars, and they're not porkers. Don't know why they bother me. They're just cars in front, heading the same way as me. Nobody staring back. So why'm I getting spun? Never mind, Bigeyes. I just am. I got a nose for grinks.

Nearest car turns left. I carry on. Other car's still in front of me. Three big gobbos crowded in the back, two more in the front. Can't make out their faces. Could be anyone. Guys cruising home from a night out. But I'm getting choked wondering.

They turn off too and I drive past.

Over the traffic lights, down past the bus station. I'm going the long way round, Bigeyes, missing out the one-way system. I want to come to South Street from behind the football stadium. It's a bit dronky cos there's lots of duffs round those streets, but it's more deserted and I'd rather meet a duff than a grink.

Here we go. Onto Cornwall Drive, round the roundabout, straight over, down Schubert Avenue. Van's rattling a bit but the gas's holding up. I've been watching the gauge, even if you haven't.

End of the road, stop, check. Left at the junction, and now we keep straight on, follow the road round. See the stadium on the right? Big dusky thing, all quiet now. Don't like this place much. Only ever come here on match days to lift wallets.

Or I used to.

Cos that's over, Bigeyes. In this city anyway.

I'm thinking of Mary now. I'm starting to see her face in my mind. I've been pushing it aside all the way here cos I was worried I might not even make it to the pub. But now we're almost there. And I'm scared in case something happens at the last minute.

Or I mess up.

But here's South Street straight ahead.

Turn off just before. We'll take this spitty little side street. It's a bit rough and narrow but we can park the van down it and come at the pub from the back. Keep off South Street altogether. Van doesn't like the potholes but we're almost there now.

Pull over, engine off, check round.

High walls, high buildings. Old houses, Bigeyes, built long before the stadium. And The Crown's ancient. They probably put that thing up before football got invented.

Out of the van, check round again.

Nobody in sight, thank Christ. There's usually some old duff slapping it under a blanket. No sign of anyone here. Okay, Bigeyes. Check out the wall on your left. That's the back of The Crown. The crumbly building beyond it's the pub.

Told you it was ancient. And the great thing about ancient buildings is they're a jink to break into. Come on, let's go find Mary. We got to get this thing sorted.

Over the wall, whack of a climb, drop down the other side. Got to tread cute now. Never been in here before. Long garden with tables and chairs, most of 'em covered up. Creep to the back door, check it over.

Easy piss, Bigeyes. Door's got a lock even you could pick. But if the drainpipe's firm, we can climb in through that upstairs window they've so kindly left open for us. Should take us straight to the bedrooms too and we won't have to fumble about on the stairs.

Drainpipe's cute. Up we go, slow, slow. I'm trying to go steady but I'm desperate to see Mary now, desperate to talk to her. I'm nervous too, Bigeyes. I don't mind admitting. I'm nervous cos I'm remembering what she said to me last time we spoke.

Here's the window. Just ajar but no problem. Ease it up, nice and quiet, slide in. Bathroom, dim, cold floor, tap dripping into the basin. Reach out, turn it off, check the door. It's half open.

Step through. Landing stretching right and left, doors all along it. Now it gets hard, Bigeyes. Cos I got no idea which one she's in. I could wake up some other neb. And waking Mary could be bad too. If I scare her, she'll scream.

Got to choose, left or right?

Left.

We'll check out the rooms closest to South Street first. Creep down, listening, listening. Car roars past the pub, doesn't stop, sound recedes. First door, closed. Doesn't feel right. Can't explain it. But Mary's not in there.

Don't ask me how I know.

Next door, next door, next door. I'm not even trying 'em, Bigeyes. They don't feel right. You're thinking this is crazy. Maybe it is. But she's not in those rooms, okay? She's just not in 'em. She's . . .

Shh! Listen.

Snoring.

Room at the end. Must be overlooking the street. And someone's in there. Least we know they're asleep. Tiptoe down, slow, slow, and I'm getting this feeling, Bigeyes.

Yeah, I know. Could be anyone. And you may be right. But I got to check. I got to do it. Walk up to the door, reach out, touch the handle, squeeze, turn. Sound of snoring stops.

I wait, take a breath, push open the door.

And see Mary's eyes staring at me.

36

SHE'S IN AN OLD SINGLE BED, propped up
with pillows so she's almost upright. Hair's hanging loose
over a dronky nightdress, torn in one sleeve. She's got her
day clothes thrown over a chair. Poky little room: rickety fur-
niture, scuffy carpet.

She looks ill.

"You look ill," she says.

I give a start. Wasn't expecting her to say that.

"Close the door," she says.

I close the door, slow, quiet. Stand there, watching her.
She's running her eyes over me. Doesn't look startled at all.
It's almost like she was expecting me.

"I was expecting you," she says.

She's freaking me out, talking like this.

"You're in danger," I mutter.

She still doesn't look startled. Seems almost amused. Then
her face softens.

"Come over here," she says.

I walk up to the bed. Her eyes are watching me close now.
I remember how they did that in the bungalow, when she
was scared I might hurt her. I hope she's not scared now. I
don't want her to be scared of me.

"I'm not scared of you," she says.

Jesus, Bigeyes. I wish she'd stop gobbing what's in my

head. It's spooking me bad. I sit down on the bed, out of reach.

"No," she says.

"No what?"

"You've got to get over this."

"Over what?"

"Being touched by a friend who means you no harm."

I don't answer, just sit there, feeling trapped. She holds out a hand. I can see it's an effort for her to lift it. I stay where I am.

"Come on," she murmurs. "Sit closer."

I move closer, just a bit. She drops her hand to the bed, gives a sigh.

"I can't hold the damn thing up in the air forever." She gives a chuckle, then turns and stretches over the other side of the bed. Pokes about a bit, like she's looking for something, then straightens up, holding a gun.

Points it at me.

"Now sit closer."

I shake my head.

"You told me it's only got blanks in it."

"Oh, damn." She clicks her tongue. "I did, didn't I?"

I can't help it, Bigeyes. I just love that Irish voice. It's like she's singing rather than talking. I mimic it back to her.

"Yeah, you did."

She raises an eyebrow.

"Please tell me that wasn't meant to be an Irish accent."

She puts down the gun, fixes her gaze on me. I hesitate, move closer. Closer again. She goes on watching me. I can see her eyes better now in the darkness. They look so weary.

"Mary?"

"Yes, my love?"

"Are you really dying?"

"I told you I was on the phone."

"Yeah, but . . . I mean . . . like . . ."

"Like now?" she says. "This very second?"

"Not this very second."

"Today then?"

She's making fun of me now. Haven't seen this side of her before. Kind of playful. But we haven't got time for that.

"Mary, listen. Listen good. You—"

"I'm not dying today."

"Mary—"

"Not planning on it anyway."

She reaches out again, stretching for my hand. I'm close enough now. She can take it if she wants to. But she doesn't. She just holds hers still. And I know what she's doing. She's meeting me halfway. But only halfway.

I got to do the rest.

Yeah, okay. I get it.

Ease my hand out, just a bit. She keeps hers still, like she's making me reach every centimeter. Christ's sake, Mary, take my bloody hand, can you? But she doesn't. She just waits, watching my face. I reach out farther, farther—take her hand.

Her fingers close round mine.

Strangely tight. For some reason they make me think of Jaz's hand. Those little fingers. I've held them too. And they scared me just as much as Mary's do.

"You're in danger, Mary. Big danger."

"Yes, yes."

She doesn't sound bothered. Just tired.

"You got to get away," I say. "Away from the city. Far away. There's people hunting me and now they're hunting you. The police want to interview you. I heard it on the news. They think you might know where I am. So these other guys'll be after you too. And they're dangerous. They're—"

"Blade." She's looking at me hard. "Listen. It doesn't matter about me. What matters is you."

"You matter too."

She shakes her head.

"It's time for you to stop running. I told you that on the phone."

"But—"

"You've done some bad things. You said so yourself. So give yourself up to the police. Take responsibility for what you've done. Pay the penalty, serve your time, start again. You're still young enough to have a future. Running's not the answer."

"But those men—"

"Never mind those men."

"They'll kill you," I say. "Maybe do something worse."

"Do you think I care?" She watches me for a moment. "Why do you think I stood up to them that time in the bungalow? And again by the warehouse. Do you think I'm naturally brave?"

"Yeah, I do."

"Well, I'm not."

She is, Bigeyes. Don't listen to her. She's brave. Trust me. She's one of the bravest people I've ever met. She was scared of me at first. And she was scared of the grinks. But she faced up to all of us and didn't flinch.

"You saved my life," I say. "And I want to save yours."

"But you can't, sweetheart." She squeezes my hand tighter. "Don't you see? I've got a week or two left. Maybe just days. I knew I was on borrowed time when I first met you. That's why it was so easy to defy those men. What can they do to me when I'm dying already?"

"Lots of things."

"Like what?"

I let go of her hand, stand up. I'm shaking but I can't help myself. I reach over to the wall, flick on the light. Mary looks up at me, blinking. I stare back at her for a moment, then tear off my coat, sweater, shirt. Turn my naked back to her. She gives a gasp.

"My God! Who did that to you? Those men?"

"Men like 'em. And there's lots of 'em. More than you ever want to meet."

She's silent. But I can feel her eyes on my back, tracing a path over the wounds Dig wanted to see. And I'm tracing 'em too, in my head. I know what they look like, every scratch. I've seen 'em enough times in snugs where there's lots of mirrors. I could draw 'em for you, Bigeyes, every detail. And I can do more.

I can remember how it felt when they cut me.

Mary speaks, quietly.

"Put your clothes back on."

I do as she says, turn off the light, stand there.

"Sit on the bed," she says. "Hold my hand again."

I do that too. We don't speak. We just sit in the darkness.

After a while I realize she's crying. I make myself squeeze her hand, like she did mine. She goes on crying for a few minutes, then pulls out a handkerchief from under the pillow and wipes her nose.

"I'm so sorry," she murmurs. "About what's happened to you."

"You're not doing so great yourself."

She strokes the top of my hand with her thumb. Feels kind of nice. She wipes her nose again.

"If I tell you about me, will you tell me about you?"

I don't answer.

"I'll tell you anyway," she says. "You can do what you like. I don't need to know anything. I'm only asking because . . . well, because I care."

I still don't answer.

Stop scowling, Bigeyes. You know why I'm not answering? Cos I can't speak, that's why. And why can't I speak? Cos I care too. You got that? I care too. So wipe that look off your face.

Mary goes on.

"I'm running from my family. Or rather, my sister." She fixes me with her eyes. "You make your friends in life, you know? But you inherit your family. If they're good, that's fine. But if they're bad, you're in trouble."

"And you're in trouble."

"Well, I was. Till I found Jacob again."

Sound of a car outside on South Street. I flick back the curtain, check it out.

"You're jumpy," she says.

"You know why."

"They're not interested in me, those men. And I told

you, I'm not bothered about them. I'm more bothered about you."

I check out the street. Car's gone past already. Didn't stop. I close the curtain again.

"Go on," I say.

37

"JACOB'S MY TWIN BROTHER," she says. "And my best friend in all the world."

"Where is he now?"

"Sleeping in the next room."

I glance toward the door.

"He won't wake up," she says. "Nothing ever wakes Jacob. He was just the same as a boy. I could fire this gun and he wouldn't hear it."

I look back at her.

"What about the other rooms?"

"Empty."

"All of 'em?"

"Yes. There's nobody else in the pub apart from you, me and Jacob."

"Does he own The Crown?"

She shakes her head.

"Friends of his do, people he used to know in Dublin. They sleep in a house down the road. Jacob helps out in the bar and restaurant and they give him free board and lodging. And me too now. For a few more days anyway."

"Do they know the police are looking for you?"

"Yes."

"Does Jacob?"

"Of course." She squeezes my hand again. "I already knew

before you got here. I listen to the radio too, you know." She leans back against the pillows, breathing hard. "That's why I knew you'd come."

"You didn't know for certain."

"Yes, I did."

"But how?"

She turns her head toward the curtains.

"Because underneath all that bravado, you've got a big heart."

I don't speak. Don't know what to say.

"You don't think so," she says, "but you have. You're worried about what you've done. You're worried about me. You've probably got other people you're worried about too."

I think about Jaz. Yeah, Bigeyes. I think about Jaz.

Mary looks back at me.

"My story's easily told. I own a farm in the south of Ireland. Just a small one but good land, great land. I inherited it from my parents and worked it all my life."

"You got a husband?"

"No. Never married, never wanted to. I hired the people I needed and Jacob's helped me a lot too. We're close, you know? Like I say, he's my best friend in all the world. He's lived with me on the farm for most of his life and the business has done well, no question. But I've got no children to leave it to."

"Can't you sell it?"

"I could." She pauses. "But I want to leave it to Jacob."

"Does he want it?"

"Yes. Very much. He loves the farm. So I've put it in the will. He'll get the farm when I die."

"So what's the problem?"

"My sister, Louisa. And her husband. And the people they hire to do their filthy work."

Another car engine outside. I don't look out this time, just listen. It's ticking over just below the window. Mary's watching me cute, saying nothing. Engine goes on ticking over, then suddenly revs up, powers off.

"Go on," I say.

She gives me a quizzical look.

"Sure you want me to?"

"Course. I want to hear."

"Louisa's the youngest of the three of us. And she's bad, really bad. Feckless, greedy, unstable, almost . . . I hate to say it . . ."

"Evil," I murmur.

"Yes, I suppose so. Jacob won't have anything to do with her, and she's always been a little scared of him. That's good in a way because with him living on the farm, it's kept her away from me too. But since Jacob left to come here, I've had no end of trouble with her."

"Why?"

"Because she wants the farm badly. She's always wanted it. Her husband's obsessed with it too. They don't need it. They're rolling in money. They already own lots of property in the area. But it's prime land and they want to exploit it."

"So what happened?"

"They started by trying to charm me into changing the will, so that Louisa would inherit the farm instead of Jacob. They argued that Jacob was too old, too much of a loner, useless at business and so on, whereas they were experienced with property management. All that stuff."

"Did you agree?"

"Of course not."

"So what happened then?"

"They kidnapped me."

"You serious?"

Mary nods.

"My illness did it. Made them desperate, I mean. It happened very suddenly. I'd been feeling poorly for a while but I hadn't said anything to anybody, then all at once I felt this terrible pain, went for some tests, and they told me it was cancer—inoperable. Got home, feeling stunned, desperate to tell Jacob. But I didn't know where he was. He'd come to this city to look up some old friends and maybe stay a few weeks. That was all I knew."

She hesitates.

"Jacob's . . . his own man. Totally independent and he just kind of assumes everyone else is like him. So he's not the kind of person to ring every five minutes. And he doesn't like mobile phones, so he hasn't got one. He said he'd get in touch with me when he had a definite address here, and I know he would have done so in time, but when this business blew up, I hadn't heard anything from him. I didn't know who his friends were either, so I couldn't get in touch with him to tell him I was ill. All I knew was that he was somewhere in this city. And I didn't want Louisa to hear about the cancer because I knew she might do something reckless. But she found out somehow. And acted at once."

Mary's face seems to darken. She looks down as if to hide it.

"They came in the middle of the night. Not Louisa or her husband. They'd never get involved personally. It was some men, faces covered. But I knew straightaway who'd sent them." She tightens her grip round my hand. "They bundled me into a van and took me to a deserted house. Kept me locked in a dark room, no windows, no food, no water, no toilet. Then they worked on me."

I can't bear this, Bigeyes. I don't want to hear any more. But she goes on.

"I won't go into details." She's speaking low, forcing the words out. "But as you can imagine, the object of the exercise was to make me change my will."

"And did you?"

"No." She looks up and there's defiance in her face. "I didn't budge."

Jesus, Bigeyes. Are you listening to this? I told you she was brave. And now I'll tell you something else. She's more than brave. She's heroic. She's got more spit than all the grinks in the world put together.

She narrows her eyes.

"And then I escaped."

38

IT'S NO GOOD, BIGEYES. I can't deal with this. She stands up to those gobbos. She gets away. She rescues herself. Then she rescues me. I'm telling you, I love this old girl. I love her to bits. I haven't got half the guts she's got.

Her eyes are bright now, steely bright.

"There was a loose floorboard," she says. "I managed to pry it up with the heel of my shoe. Then I rammed the end of the board at the door handle. I had to keep jabbing at it but the lock mechanism was quite flimsy and eventually I broke it and got out."

"What about the gobbos?"

"The what?"

"The men."

"They weren't there. They'd gone outside for a breather or a cigarette or something. It was still the middle of the night. They obviously didn't expect me to get out and just left me in there with the door locked. I presume they were intending to come back but I didn't see them at all when I finally made it downstairs."

"What did you do then?"

"I ran. Well, as much as a sick old woman can run."

"To the police?"

She shakes her head.

"I had no proof of who my attackers were. No faces, no names. And nothing concrete against Louisa and her husband. The most I could have claimed would have been that some men I couldn't identify had tried to force me to change my will in favor of my sister. I knew that wouldn't constitute evidence. I also knew Louisa would try to get at me again."

"So you came here. To the city."

"Yes. Since I've only got a short time to live. All I wanted to do was find Jacob and keep away from Louisa's thugs. The will's safe. Jacob'll get the farm."

"Won't she just try it on with him?"

"What, you mean the charm and the intimidation?"

"Yeah."

"No, because it won't work. Jacob's not scared of her. He's not scared of anybody. And he's got nothing but contempt for Louisa, especially after what's happened to me. He'll leave the farm to anybody in the world but her. And she knows that."

Mary pauses, goes on.

"But the thing is—while all this drama was going on, Jacob knew nothing about it, and I was desperate to tell him. And spend my last days with him. He's all I've got left."

She looks at me strangely for a moment.

"Well, almost."

I'm not sure what that means.

She strokes my hand again.

"I haven't acted . . . legally," she says. "I've misled the police, given a false name and address, used someone else's bungalow. But the thing is . . . I had so little time. And I don't want to spend my last precious hours talking to police officers. I want to spend them with Jacob."

She gives me that strange look again.

"Though it seems," she adds, "that I'm destined to spend some of them with you."

"I'm sorry," I say.

"I'm not," she answers.

Silence. I feel kind of awkward. She doesn't speak. So I do.

"How did you get back to the farm after you broke out of the house?"

"I told you. I ran. Luckily it wasn't too far. The farm was empty when I got there but I knew I wouldn't have long before they came for me again. I splashed my face, changed my clothes and got my father's old gun from the drawer."

She picks it up, turns it over.

"He only ever used it to scare off the crows. Used to fire blanks up into the air."

She puts it down again.

"I took the gun and some blanks, scraped together a few personal things, then left. Made one big cash withdrawal from the hole in the wall in town, then headed off to catch the ferry to England. I haven't made any withdrawals since. I don't want to be traced."

She shivers for a moment.

"Because I'll tell you something—while I'm still alive, Louisa will go on looking. She doesn't know I'm staying with Jacob but even if she's guessed that, she'll keep searching. You remember those three heavies who burst in on us in the bungalow?"

"Yeah."

"My first thought was that it was Louisa's men. It never occurred to me they were looking for you."

If only I'd known, Bigeyes. Christ, I could have helped her. I should have helped her. Why didn't I? And now I'm too late.

She looks at me, smiles, and I can see she's reading my mind again.

"You couldn't have helped me," she says. "You had enough on your plate. But I'll tell you something. That time in the bungalow, when I offered you—"

"A hundred quid."

"Yes." She frowns. "I can't tell you how glad I was when you turned it down. That was pretty much all I had left."

But she still offered it, Bigeyes. You cracking this? She still bloody offered it. I'm guilting up big-time. I force myself to speak.

"How did you find Jacob?"

"He'd told me his friends ran a pub or a bistro or something. He wasn't quite sure of the details. Typical Jacob. He just had their phone number, which of course he didn't think to give to me. So I ended up trawling round every pub, bar and bistro I could get to. And there are hundreds in this city."

She takes a long, tired breath.

"I was getting close to despair. I can't walk much now and I could feel my energy draining away. When I found you lying outside the warehouse, I was checking some of the pubs down by the river. And that's when the miracle happened. Maybe it was a little gift from Providence for helping you. I don't know."

"What do you mean?"

"I went with you to the hospital and while they were operating on you, I met Jacob. There, of all places."

"In the hospital?"

"Yes."

Outside on the street I catch another engine. Smoother

than the others. A sleek, purry motor. Mary takes no notice of it.

"He'd just been to Emergency. Can you believe it? Cut his hand with a kitchen knife and wanted it properly bandaged. We caught sight of each other at the very same moment. It was just . . . too good to be true."

Engine's getting louder. Why'm I scared, Bigeyes? Could be anybody. The other motors weren't a problem. Maybe this one won't be either. But I'm still scared. Mary speaks.

"I was hoping you'd tell me about yourself."

She lowers her voice.

"But I can see there's no time now. Because you're leaving, aren't you?"

The engine draws closer. It's just a short way off now. Can't see the car. Don't need to. It pulls over outside the pub. Engine falls quiet. Sound of a car door, another. Mary speaks again, softly.

"I understand."

"Do you?"

"Yes."

She holds my eyes.

"You want to lead them away. So they don't hurt me."

She's right, Bigeyes. I don't want 'em to hurt her. I don't want anyone to hurt her. She leans forward suddenly, pulls me close, holds me. I feel her body shake.

"Take care of yourself," she murmurs. "And forget about me."

"I won't. Ever."

"Forget about me. Now go."

She pushes me back. I look at her. I'm shaking too but I can't stop it. I want something I didn't think I could ever want. I want her to hold me again. She looks at me, understands, pulls me close again. I hold her back, tight.

Footsteps in the street, low voices.

I recognize one straight up.

The grunt.

Mary kisses me on the cheek, pushes me away again. I stand up, look down at her. It's the last time I'll ever see her. I know it. And she knows it too.

"I love you, Mary," I mutter.

She gives me a smile: a soft, sweet smile like I never had before.

"I know you do, darling," she says.

I hold her eyes a moment longer, then turn to the door.

And I'm gone.

39

DOWN THE CORRIDOR, tracking the sounds. Yeah, Bigeyes, I'm blasted in my head but I can still think. And I'm thinking just one thing right now.

Get those grinks away from Mary.

Doesn't matter about me. But I got to look after Mary. Like I got to look after Jaz. They're all I care about now. They're all that's worth caring about.

Footsteps in the street, tripping slow. I can hear 'em good, even from inside the pub. They've split. Grunt's gone right, other grink's gone left. I'm sure of it. I can hear the fat man's step easy. Plunk plunk plunk. He probably thinks he's creeping.

Other gobbo's gone quiet. Can't make out where he is. Wait a second. . . .

Got him. Shuffly little step and it's already gone quiet again—but I know where he is now. He's down by the chip shop. I'm thinking hard, Bigeyes. Somehow I got to climb out, get to Dig's van, drive off, make 'em see me, make 'em follow.

Cos I'm the one they want. And there's still a chance they don't even know Mary's in here. Some screamer's tipped 'em off but it might be just me they saw. Hope so. Long as Mary stays safe, that's cute. But I still got to lead 'em away.

And now I got another idea.

Forget the drainpipe and back garden.

211

We'll use the front door. More risky but it's the grunt who's nearest and I could run round him on one leg. Down the corridor, top of the stairs, stop. Silence now, inside, outside, everywhere. Just the sound of my breathing, and my thoughts, loud in my head.

I can still see Mary's door. Closed, like I left it. But I can picture her inside. She's lying there, tense, worrying. I know she is. She's worrying herself sick about me. I got to go, got to get myself out of her head. And keep her safe.

Down the stairs, up to the front door, listen again. No sounds outside but I got to move now, whatever happens. If they know I'm in here, they'll be phoning for help. If they're here on a hunch, I still got a chance.

Push up the mail slot, peer out. No sign of anyone, just the dark street and the car they parked there. Big, shiny bastard, cool shit. Nobody in it. Okay, so there's two of 'em. And one's the fat man.

Sound of footsteps plodding close. It's the grunt coming back. Ease the mail slot down again, listen on. He blobs past, walks on to join his mate. But the other guy's moving too. I can hear him. He's left the chippo and he's walking back.

Footsteps stop. Sound of talking over to the left, the grunt again and this time I catch the other voice. I know this gobbo. I've heard him talk before. Lenny, that's his name. Mean dronk, one of Paddy's old crew.

I know what I got to do. I know exactly. But I got to play stealth. Got to make 'em see me, but not coming out of the pub, like there's no connection. They got to see me some other way. But I can't move till I know which way they're going.

If they head this way again, I'm blitzed. If they go the other way . . .

They're moving.

Listen, wait. Still talking but the voices are fading. So are the footsteps. They're heading left. They're heading the other way. It's got to be now. I won't get a better chance.

Open the front door, soft as I can. I'm begging it not to click. It doesn't, thank Christ. Peep round into the street. Both gobbos down by the chippo. They've stopped walking, but they got their backs to me.

Ease the door closed. Again it doesn't click. What a beauty. Keep my eyes on the grinks. They're still facing the other way, talking low. Grunt's pulled out a flashlight and he's shining it down the little alleyway next to the chippo.

Slip down South Street, away from the grinks. Keep close to the buildings, check over my shoulder. They haven't turned yet. Yeah, boys. Keep popping your heads into that alleyway. On, on, toward the end of South Street, and still they haven't turned.

Just a bit farther. Creep on, hugging the shadows, and now we're there. End of South Street just ahead, Wistler Road cutting off to the right. It takes us round the back of these buildings and joins up with the little side street where I left the van.

Slip into the doorway of the bank, check round.

They've moved away from the chippo. They're out in the middle of South Street looking up at the pub. Christ, Big-eyes, I hope Mary hasn't put her light on or something. They got to think there's no one awake right now.

And they got to see me.

Like I'm coming from somewhere else.

It's now or never.

Step out of the doorway, walk into South Street like I'm crossing it from Wistler Road, going somewhere else. Wait for the shout.

Nothing.

Christ, boys, wake up. Then I hear it.

"There!"

The grunt's voice. And now a thunder of footsteps. I stop, check round, make like I'm surprised. I got to do this right. If I duck straight down Wistler Road, one of 'em'll come on and the other'll cut back and come at me from the side street. I'll never make it to Dig's van.

I got to hesitate a bit, make 'em both come on, then blast down Wistler Road. I need 'em on my butt, both of 'em, not coming from opposite directions. But I can't let 'em get too close either. Lenny looks quick and you already know I'm not fast.

I run across the road, like I'm heading for the gate into the park, stop, dither, change my mind, run on, dither again, run back toward Wistler Road. They're coming on fast, 'specially Lenny, but I still need 'em closer. They mustn't split and plug me from two sides.

I make myself trip, roll on the ground, pick myself up again, and now it's time. Shit, it's time. I might have left it too late. They're pumping hard, eyes gleaming with triumph.

Dive into Wistler Road.

I've left it too late. They're much too close. I can hear Lenny's breath jerking out of him, the grunt heaving just behind. Tear down Wistler Road, right into the little side street, down that, pelting, panting, checking round.

Grunt's pulled up, gasping, but Lenny's coming on, and he's gaining. Two duffs in the shadows ahead, digging in one of the bins. Lenny blares at 'em.

"He's got my wallet! Hundred quid each if you stop him!"

They straighten up, look at each other, edge across my path. I run to the right, pick up an old crate, throw it at 'em. One of the duffs moves back, other stands his ground.

"Stop him!" shouts Lenny.

The duff comes forward. Moves slow, scabby on his feet. I grab one of the bins. Empty, thank God. Pick it up, fling it at him. Thumps into the ground close by him. Duff moves back and I'm past, but I've lost time and Lenny's closer.

Much closer.

I'm not going to make it to the van. No way.

Another duff in front of me, an old gobbo, lurching, bottle in each hand. He's staring up at the sky, murmuring to the night. Don't think he's even seen me. Lenny calls out again.

"Stop that kid! He's nicked my wallet! Hundred quid if you stop him!"

Gobbo goes on talking to the sky. I'm on him before he knows it, snatch the bottles, pull him round so he's between me and Lenny. Lenny clatters into him and they both fall to the ground.

Race on toward the van. I can see it now, just a short way down, and there on the right's the back of The Crown. Light on in one of the upstairs windows. Two figures standing there. Mary and a gobbo. Got to be Jacob.

They've seen me.

Jacob's talking into a phone.

But I got no time for that. Lenny's coming on again, faster than ever. Sound of a car revving up on South Street. Grunt must have turned back for the motor. I got seconds, that's all, seconds before he drives round and heads me off.

Up to the van, fumble for the keys.

Got 'em. Jerk open the door, check round. Lenny's storming in. I hurl the bottles at him. He dodges one, catches the other, comes on. I jump in the van, lock the door, crunch the key in the ignition, turn it, pray.

Engine mutters, mutters, mutters.

Start, you dingo!

It fires. I rev up, hard. Clutch down, first gear.

Thump against the driver's door. Lenny's there, face against the window. He's clutching at the van, swearing, spitting, belting hate. I start to drive but he goes on clinging there, pounding the side. I speed up.

Crash! The side window shatters and glass comes flying through. He's punched the bottle into it and smashed his way in. His hand's dripping blood from the broken glass but he's grabbing at my throat.

I step on the accelerator and he falls off the van. I see him in the mirror, rolling on the ground. Up through the gears, fast as I can. Got to get out of this street before the grunt drives in. But I'm too late. There's headlights in front of me.

Bearing down.

40

OKAY, FAT MAN. If that's what you want. Flick on the headlights, full beam. Jam on the horn, ram the accelerator into the floor. Steer straight at him. Yeah, claphead, I'm ready to blow blood. Are you?

He's not. He swerves to the side like a dimp. I scream past, scraping his shiny toy on the way. His eyes meet mine—just for a second—and then I'm gone. Out onto South Street, right, then left. Away down Tannery Lane.

And here come the grinks, quick as wind, tires squealing as they chase my tail. They didn't lose a second. I'll say that for 'em. Must have jetted down Wistler Road and out that way. Check the mirror. Grunt's driving, Lenny's wrapping something round his cut hand.

No other motors in sight yet. Why not? And why's Lenny not ringing for help? Never mind his cut. He should be ringing for help first. But I think I get it. I can see it in their faces. They want me bad, they want me so bad. And they want me for themselves. This is personal.

And that's fine with me. Cos there's something they've forgotten, Bigeyes. Something maybe you've forgotten. This is my turf. Yeah, Bigeyes, my turf, my home ground. Not theirs, not yours, but mine. And you know what? I've had enough of running from scum. These two want me for themselves? Well, let's see, let's find out.

Who's chasing who?

Who's going to win?

Gas is the big problem. Needle's right down now. Maybe won't have enough to get back to the prof's house. But I can still crack these grinks. Long as I got enough juice to get where I want to go. And the porkers stay back.

We'll take the side streets.

Left onto Morris Lane, right at the end, down to the market, onto Copeland Drive. Grinks still hot behind. Grunt's driving well. Can't say he's not. He moves like a pudding but he knows how to handle a motor. I'm not going to outrun 'em in this van.

But I don't want to. Not now.

Over the cobblestones, left onto Cartmel Lane, left again, right onto Beaston Road. Check the mirror. Still on my tail, close as before. I can see the grunt leaning over the wheel, hunched like a bear.

Yeah, big man. I can feel your breath, your foul, grunty breath. And that's cute. I need you right where you are, you and your mate. Close, real close. I see the grunt's eyes harden. They've caught sight of me watching in the mirror.

I give him a smirk, then wheel right.

Down onto King Street, right at the end, right again and down onto Bellevue Parade. Got to watch it now. Big, big road and there's bound to be porkers here. But I got to take this one. If I had more juice, we could go round, but I can't risk it.

Check round. Cars heading both ways, lots of 'em, but I think we're cute. They're all muffins. I can tell. No porkers, no grinks. I watch 'em pass by. It's like they're floating, like they're from another world.

A world I can't have.

A safe world.

Bang! Van gives a jolt. Check the mirror. Grunt's nudged me up the bum. Thought he might try that. Yeah, dungpot, you're trying to blam me off to the side, maybe nip a tire, make me pull over. Won't work. Cos we're turning off here.

Left down the slip road, up to the roundabout, down into the underpass, through it and up again. Lights of the city below: streets, houses, shops, factories. Bastard river snaking off to the right. And in my mirror, the grinks pushing close.

I squeeze the steering wheel.

"It's time, boys."

Left down the exit road, right onto Waldegrave Avenue, down to the bottom, right onto Musgrave Road, and there it is at the end. Got it, Bigeyes? Stockland Heights. The big, black building at the end. It's a block of flats. Only there's no lights on in any of 'em. Know why?

Cos no one lives there.

Not even duffs.

You'll soon see why.

Slow down, sharp. Got to make 'em brake quick. No sweat if they ram me again, long as they don't stuff the van. But he's quick, that grunt. He's braked straight up and he's watching cute.

Wondering what I'm doing.

Got to make him think, Bigeyes. Got to speed up, slow down, mess about. Get a bit of distance before I bail out. If he's too close, I won't make it into the flats. But it's working. He's hesitating, just a bit. Thinks I'm maybe going to wig it from here.

Slow down again. Got to make him stop, but not in front of me. Mustn't let him cut me off. He's hanging back, like he's wary. Good boy, stay where you are.

Stop the van, check the mirror.

He pulls up, just behind. Lenny gets out, grunt stays at the wheel. Lenny starts walking forward. I rev up, power off.

That's it. Only chance I'll get. I got my foot hard down and I'm ripping through the gears. Check behind. Lenny's back in the car and they're coming on fast. But I've creamed some time off 'em.

Just hope it's enough.

Screech up to Stockland Heights, brake hard. Van squeals round and comes to a halt. Grinks are racing in too but I'm out of the van and in through the entrance by the time I hear the clunk of their doors.

Up the stairs, dark all around. Glass crunching underfoot, smell of piss and beer. Sound of feet pounding on the steps behind me. I run on, up, up, fast as I can, quiet and loud at the same time. Quiet so they think I'm trying to escape.

Loud so they hear me.

Yeah, Bigeyes, they got to hear me. They got to know where I am.

Cos I'm going to finish this now.

41

UP, UP, FLOOR AFTER FLOOR. There's eight of
'em and we got to run up the lot. Grinks are still pounding
after me but I got to play this cute like before. Got to make
sure they find me together. If the grunt's hanging back cos
he's bombed, it won't work.

It might not work anyway.

I'm banging everything on one throw.

Run on, listening hard. Lighter steps closer up, thumpy
ones farther down. Grunt's starting to struggle. I got to
think, Bigeyes. Got to make the fat man catch up. But there's
no time here.

Lenny's too close. If I stick here, he'll get me.

Up, up, breathing hard now. I'm bombed out too, and I
got Mary's face choking my mind, and Jaz's face, and sweet
Becky's face. The Becky who died. That's there too. They're
watching me, all three of 'em.

As I run on up the stairs.

Fourth floor, fifth floor, sixth floor. Lenny's still close but
the grunt's gone quiet. I'm in the grime now. But I still can't
stop. Got to keep climbing.

Grunt's started moving again. I can hear him. I reckon
he's two floors down. I got to keep out of Lenny's way for a
bit, let the fat man catch up.

Seventh floor.

Check round. Thump of footsteps still behind. Stairs

ahead up to the top floor, corridor down to the right. Check again. There's still no time. I got to go on up. And if Lenny gets there on his own, keep out of the way somehow, till the grunt joins him.

Up the steps, quiet now, soft as I can. Into the top-floor corridor. Creep down, slow, slow. Rooms on either side. No doors anywhere. Been kicked in ages ago. Just shells here: black, smelly, paint-sprayed shells. It's like you're walking through a death's head.

And maybe I am.

Gone quiet behind me. That's good. Means Lenny's not sure, so he's thinking. That'll give Grunty time to reach him. Creep on. I know the room I want. I know it well. The room at the end. Best room in the block once.

But you wouldn't want to live there now.

Sound of footsteps again—two sets. They're coming up the stairs, both gobbos together. And that's cute. I need 'em to find me now. Stop, check round. I'm halfway down the corridor. Couple more seconds and they'll be through that door.

And then they'll see me. Like I want 'em to. But I'm shaking, Bigeyes. I'm breathing blood and I'm shaking. Cos this is it. Them or me.

There they are, in the doorway. Lenny and the grunt. I can't see their faces in the darkness, just the shape of 'em. They move down the corridor like walking shadows.

I stand there, watch, think. I got to do this right. If I mess up, it's over. Look right, left, like I'm checking rooms. Look back at the grinks. They're coming on, slow, steady, sure of themselves. Check the rooms again.

Turn and start to run.

Toward the room at the end.

No sound of running from the grinks. They're taking it slow, real slow. No rush now. They know I can't get out.

Stop, check some of the other doors, look round again. Grinks are closer, much closer. Now they've speeded up. You know why?

Cos they can't wait, Bigeyes.

That's why.

And neither can I. I run on, down to the room at the end, stop in the open doorway. From inside comes a shiver of light. It's coming from the moon. It's reaching down and trickling in through the empty space that used to be the door to the balcony.

I turn back to the grinks, snarl at 'em.

"Which one of you wants to die first?"

They stop, both faces clear now, then laugh.

"Got your knife on you?" mocks Lenny.

"Yeah."

"Let's see it then."

I push a hand into my coat pocket. The grinks watch. But they're only wary for a moment. Something tells me they know I haven't got one. The grunt smiles.

"You must have left it behind, kid."

I pull my empty hand out. Lenny smiles, then pulls out a knife of his own. The grunt pulls out a gun.

"Time to come home, little boy," says Lenny.

"Piss off!"

I turn and run into the flat. The grinks follow, taking their time again. I edge over to the far wall, feel my way round it, watching 'em close. They track me with their eyes. The grunt waves me toward the door with his gun.

"You're going the wrong way, kid."

"Piss off, fat man!"

I see him flinch. I go on feeling round the wall, closer, closer to the balcony door. Lenny shakes his head.

"No way out there."

I take no notice, move slowly on.

"I'm getting tired of this," says the grunt.

"Then have a lie-down, fat man!"

He flinches again, raises the gun. I make a face at him.

"But you can't, can you, fat boy? Can't kill me. Cos you're not allowed to. You been told to bring me in."

"I can do what I like with you," says the grunt.

"You'll have to get me first, fat arse."

He lunges forward, but I dart to the left, out onto the balcony. The moonlight's bright upon it now. I can see the city lights again, spread out below. Edge round the side of the balcony, close to the rail, watching the door.

The grunt appears first, Lenny close behind.

Not close enough. I need 'em together, not one in front. Grunt stops, looks over at me. I'm on the far side of the balcony now, back to the rail, grinks still in the doorway. The moonlight's so bright on their faces they look like ghosts.

I check out Lenny. He's still just behind the fat man. I got to do something about that. I need 'em together. I give him a little wink.

"Got no idea, have you, Lenny? How to hold a knife."

He stiffens. I spit on the balcony floor.

"You're just a paid slug. No brains, no class."

He takes a step forward, next to the grunt. And that's it, Bigeyes. Now's the time. I lean forward, crow at 'em.

"You're dregs, both of you! You can't kill me cos you've

been told you got to bring me in. But you can't even do that." I give 'em the finger. "Cos you're dumb shit!"

They don't speak. They just rush forward.

I grab the balcony rail and cling on. It happens so fast I don't have time to think. There's a crumbling sound, a groan of timbers. The frame of the balcony judders, holds firm—but the floor gives way and both men vanish from view, like the moonlight's swallowed 'em.

I hang there, listening. Not a sound from either, not even a shout. Just a slow, heavy silence.

And a moment later, two soft thuds far below.

42

Van runs out of juice half a mile from the old prof's house. Didn't think it'd make it this far. Pull over to the side of the road, slump back in the driver's seat.

I can't stop shaking. Body's tense like it's never been. It's not those grinks. I don't give two bells about them. I didn't even check their bodies. It's all this other stuff. The stuff in my head. I got to think, Bigeyes.

Got to make up my mind.

Cos I'm cracking my brain. I got thoughts buzzing, feelings buzzing. I can't believe no one stopped me on the way here. I was driving like a dimp and I passed enough porkers. There's more out now than ever. And they must know about the van. Mary's bound to have rung 'em. Or Jacob has.

But I got here. Don't ask me how.

Out of the van, start walking. Might help, might straighten me out. Keep well back from the road. Yeah, Bigeyes, I'm not a total dronk. That part of me's still working.

Walk, walk, walk.

Feels good, feels better. No cars yet either. I'll slip out of the way if I hear one. Walk on, think, try and think. Cos the thing is, Bigeyes, this is the moment. The crossroads. I knew that all the way back. It's been blitzing my head since those grinks fell from the balcony.

No, longer than that. Maybe since Mary talked to me on

the phone. Maybe even longer. I got a feeling this goes right back through Mary, through Jaz, and all the way to Becky.

The Becky who should have lived.

Cos that's the crack of it, Bigeyes. There's too many nebs should have lived and didn't. And so many of 'em died cos of me. How many more's going to die if I stay free? I don't like to think about it. And there's people I care about now.

I don't want them to suffer.

Car coming, other side. I can see the headlights. Step off the road, crouch in the shadows. Car fizzes past. Out again, walk on.

See what I mean, Bigeyes?

That's my life. Creeping in and out of shadows. Ducking, dodging. I don't know if I can do that anymore. I thought I could get away and play dead all over again. Now I'm not so sure. Not if I end up shaking like this, choked out of my head.

Mary's right. Running's not the answer.

So I've made up my mind.

I'm telling Dig thanks but no. He doesn't have to help me get away. Cos I'm giving myself up. I'll tell him he's got half an hour to clear his gang out of the prof's house and then I'm ringing the porkers from there.

And I'll wait for 'em to come and get me.

Yeah, I know. Doesn't solve very much. Cos my enemies are still out there. And they'll find a way of getting at me in prison. There's too much stuff they want from me. There's retribution to pay too. I guess I won't live that long.

But I don't know if staying free's any better. And there's one other thing. One big thing. I'll be able to look Becky's spirit in the eye and not be so ashamed. And Mary's too when she dies.

And little Jaz.

I might even be able to face her too.

And that's why I'm going back to the prof's house first. I could have gone straight to the porkers but I gave a promise. To myself anyway. I'm going to finish that story for Jaz.

And then say good-bye.

So there you go, Bigeyes. Crossroads over. Walking's done it for me, and talking to you. Never thought you'd turn out to be useful. But you're starting to surprise me. And now here's another crossroads. A real one with a pub. Recognize it?

The Queen Anne.

Check round. All still. I'm glad about that. Not a single car since that other one. Everything's quiet, except . . .

Sound of sirens far away in the city center.

Yeah, long way off. Just hope they're chasing someone else.

Over the crossroads, past the turning, up the lane toward the prof's house. Still quiet. Walk slow, walk careful. Riff's motor's exactly where it was. On, closer, house still dark, no lights at all. Looks just like it did when I left it.

Sky's lighter though, just a bit. Moon's still out but it's hidden by a cloud, and dawn's coming, soft and clear. Walk on, slow like before, checking round. Feels cute, feels okay.

So why'm I still shaking?

Stop, listen. Not a sound. Just the sirens again, way off, like little waily voices, nothing to do with me. Check the house again. Still feels okay but I'm shaking worse than I was. And I don't know why.

Walk on, round the side of the house, stop at the back

door, listen again. Still silence. Try the handle—unlocked. Like it was when I left. Open, step inside, close the door. Silence everywhere. And then I get it.

Everything's wrong. Don't ask me how I know. I just do. I don't need to see anything. I can feel it like a frost. I want to run. I don't want to face it. But I know I must. Even if it's a trap, I got to do it for Jaz.

Down the hall, into the lounge, kitchen, dining room. No one downstairs. Stop, take a breath, back to the hall, up the stairs. Still too quiet. Nobody on the landing. Nobody in the bedrooms. Nobody in the bathroom. I got fear pumping now. Cos I'm telling you, Bigeyes, there's bad shit here. And I'm terrified for Jaz.

Only one room left, far end of the landing. The old prof's study. I used to go in there and read. Used to sit at his big old desk and pull down his books about Descartes and Kant and Sartre and all those clever gobbos, and try and understand.

What's waiting in that room now?

Walk down, slow, eyes on the door. It's closed. Stop outside, wait, listen. Not a sound inside, nothing I can hear anyway. Look down.

There's blood trickling out of the room.

Step back, kick the door open, burst in. Dig's slumped against the wall, plugged with his own knife. There's nobody else here. I run forward, kneel down. But there's nothing I can do for him. He's finished. Then I hear it.

A whimper, close by. Can't see anyone. Another whimper. Check round and there she is, curled under the desk.

"Bex!"

She doesn't move, just curls up even more.

"Bex."

She stays where she is, moaning now. I reach in, stroke her arm. She turns her face toward me, but she's got her eyes glazed.

"Bex, what happened?"

She doesn't answer. Don't think she's even heard me. But I'm wrong. She fixes me suddenly, starts mumbling.

"Xennie was acting weird. Wouldn't talk to nobody. Just kept wandering about the house and checking her mobile. And then . . . then . . ."

"What?"

"It happened so quick. Riff calls up the stairs and says Xennie's legged it. He's seen her out the window, climbing over the fence and running off down the field. And he says there's guys down the end of the lane, hanging about where we left the motors, and more guys coming toward the house."

Bex shivers.

"Me and Dig had no chance. The others was all downstairs again but me and Dig was up here. We'd just got dressed again. And Jaz—"

"What?" I grab Bex by the shoulder. "Tell me about Jaz."

"She'd come up to look for us. When Riff called out, I was at the top of the stairs with her, giving her a cuddle. Next moment them guys come rushing in. Big heavy guys like we can't handle."

I take a slow breath.

"What happened?"

She doesn't answer.

"Bex! What happened?"

She shivers again.

"Dig shouts down to the others. Tells 'em to split. Don't know if they got away, but I think so. I heard 'em climbing out the downstairs windows and running for the fence, the way Xennie went. And the guys in the house didn't go after 'em. They caught sight of me and Jaz up on the landing and come pouring up."

I know why, Bigeyes. Christ, I know why.

Bex wipes her eyes with the back of her hand.

"Dig stood his ground. Backed us in here and tried to stop 'em. But what could he do? Eh?" She glares at me. "Nothing. They just went for him and . . ."

She bursts into tears, talking wild.

"And I didn't do shit! I'm like . . . I'm crawling under the desk with Jaz and . . . I'm holding my hands over her ears and hugging her close so she can't hear nothing, can't see nothing, and then . . . and then . . ."

"Easy, Bex."

"They all crowd round the desk, and one of 'em bends down and looks me in the face. And before I can stop him, he reaches out and pulls Jaz from me, and hands her over to some other guy, and suddenly she's gone."

"Jesus."

"She's gone!" Bex clutches at me. "And I'm screaming after her. I'm just . . . screaming. . . ."

She lets go of me, presses her face into her hands, then suddenly takes 'em away and looks back. And there's hatred in her face. Hatred for me.

"The guy reaches out again." Her voice is bubbling with rage. "And he clamps his hand over my mouth so I can't scream no more, and he's holding me tight, so tight it hurts. And I'm shaking like I never done before. And then he leans in close and he talks to me soft, yeah? Like we're mates. Calls me sweetheart. Says I got nice hair. Says if he was a bit younger, he'd ask me on a date. And then he gives me this little wink, all smooth, and he says . . ."

"I know what he says, Bex. I can guess."

"Well, I don't care!" She glowers at me. "Cos you're going to hear it anyway, you bastard!" She leans closer, spits out the words. "He says . . . tell Blade if he wants the little girl back, he knows where to come."

And she bursts into tears again.

I stand up, walk to the window, stare out over the garden. Dawn's coming faster than I thought. The moon's clear again and there's a tinge of gray on the horizon. Bex goes on crying and I want to cry too. I want to cry so much. But all I can do is listen to her. And the scream of thoughts in my head.

And the sound of police sirens.

Drawing close.